Her neck was Modigliani and the rest of her pure Neanderthal. The flat nose and large mouth in the sketch could have belonged to no one but Mrs. Patch. The rope around her throat and the distended eyes and tongue showed that she had been hanged by her neck until dead.

When it actually happened, though, it happened differently. Her head was lying on the desk, her hands oustretched as if she were taking a brief nap, and her skull was crushed. Not even the standard Atlanta cure-all of two aspirins and a Coke could help her any longer. . . .

It is always hard to believe that someone you like or someone you love can kill, however much the victim may deserve to be killed. But certainly someone at the Social Service Bureau had murdered Mrs. Patch.

Who? Bea, the girl to whom everything happened? Once she had been bitten by a mad dog. Once a client, old Mr. Smith, had talked to her quietly and then had grabbed a butcher knife and had chased her up and down stairs until he came to.

Mary? Miss Mary, the gentle, tender one? Only the week before, a telegram had

(continued on back flap)

❦ ❦ ❦ Her neck was Modigliani and the rest of her pure Neanderthal. The flat nose and large mouth in the sketch could have belonged to no one but Mrs. Patch. The rope around her throat and the distended eyes and tongue showed that she had been hanged by her neck until dead.

When it actually happened though, it happened differently. Her head was lying on the desk, her hands outstretched as if she were taking a brief nap and her skull was crushed. Not even the standard Atlanta cure-all of two aspirins and a Coke could help her any longer. . . .

It is always hard to believe that someone you like or someone you love can kill, however much the victim may deserve to be killed. But certainly someone at the Social Service Bureau had murdered Mrs. Patch.

Who? Bea, the girl to whom everything happened?

Mary? Miss Mary, the gentle, tender one?

Smitty, the career girl?

Gwen, whom everyone liked most?

Or one of the others? Peg, Margy, Miss Reeves, someone in the Children's Division, Mrs. Martin . . . who?

Who indeed would have also tried to kill Miss Fitzpatrick, poor half-crazy woman that she was? Or old Mr. Ricks, who came every day to the Bureau just to sit and watch suspiciously . . .

But someone had tried, and come close. And was almost to succeed before Jane Wallace began to sense the truth.

By turns violent, tender, intense, and humorous, this is a mystery that is at all times original and arresting. We think you will mark it down as one of the best of 1952.

MOUSE

IN

ETERNITY

N E D R A   T Y R E

NEW YORK

Alfred A. Knopf 1952

L. C. Catalog Card No. 51-11976

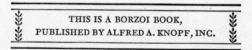

THIS IS A BORZOI BOOK,
PUBLISHED BY ALFRED A. KNOPF, INC.

Published March 10, 1952
Second printing, April 1952

When I measure myself by the grasses
Then I am good and tall;
When I measure myself by the mountains
I do not exist at all.

It is very, very curious
How one may either be
A cat that nibbles a moment,
Or a mouse in eternity.

PAULA LECLER

MOUSE

IN

ETERNITY

Mouse in Eternity

THE cold November rain hit hard against the windows. Peg squinted and looked down on Whitehall Street from the third story of the Social Service Bureau. The sad Monday morning procession started; clients swarmed below, pushing through the swinging front doors. Social workers dodged in and out of the crowd trying to get to work on time.

"Here comes Mr. Ricks," Peg said. "The week has officially begun."

I joined her at the window. Our perspective distorted everyone; we looked down directly on heads with no bodies. Every now and then large feet darted out to carry the heads forward. On the corner Mr. Ricks, who got Old Age Assistance from the Bureau, looked at the traffic light with the same suspicion he looked at women, especially women who were social workers, Republicans, politicians, and the people he referred to in a vague, general way as All them that's runnin' and ruinin' the country. The light changed. He watched it without trust as if it might turn back at once to red; a few cautious steps took him to the middle of the street, then he ran to the curb. He had gained another small victory over the world and its perverse ways.

Peg walked to her desk. She lit a cigarette, then came back near me and peered out of the window again. "There's Mary," she said. "She shouldn't be coming back to work so soon. I went by her house last night. She's paralyzed with grief."

Soon, one by one, the workers would enter the stalls, which was what we called the slim partitions where our desks were placed; four stalls on one side of the huge office, four on the other. The desks were clear; in a few moments they would be piled high with case records, clothing orders, check lists, change-of-address forms, incoming and outgoing mail.

As the workers in our section entered with a greeting I thought of a theater program, the way it deftly places everything and everyone. I went ahead with the thought; my usual Monday morning reluctance to get started helped me with the idea.

TIME: *November*. PLACE: *Social Service Bureau, Atlanta, Georgia.* CHARACTERS, *in order of their appearance*:

First, discovered as the curtain rises, Pegeen Kelly and Jane Wallace, social workers, whittling time away with small chores and small talk before the new week began.

Enter Beatrice Shaw, called Bea, the girl to whom everything happened. She would go out calmly like the rest of us to make home visits and come back with startling tales. Once she was bitten by a mad dog and had to have anti-rabies treatment. Twice she had acted as *accoucheuse*. Once a client, old Mr. Smith, had talked to her quietly and then had grabbed a butcher knife and had chased her up and down stairs. After an hour or two of this he came to and begged her to pay no attention to what he had done. "I certainly didn't mean no harm," he said, "was just one of my spells." After that when anything happened to us or among us that was somehow unaccountable or without tact we said: "I certainly didn't mean no harm, was just one of my spells."

When Bea went on leave in the summer she had said she was going to Oregon. While she waited for her train at the Terminal she had met a sailor's wife with five children on their way to Key West; the wife needed help traveling with the children, so Bea went to Key West instead of Oregon. Her latest adventure involved two black French poodles. Two weeks ago she had come back to the office from a visit leading a tandem of French poodles, named Joe and Bill. All that afternoon they did their tricks for us, a prodigious repertory. As night approached their housing became an acute problem; Bea couldn't take them to her attic apartment, so she farmed them out to Peg. Peg was the one among us who always obliged. The walls of Bea's partition were covered with Low's cartoons; she looked at them with wonder, then pulled a slender book from a desk drawer, *British Cartoonists*, by David Low; she glanced at her watch, measuring the time she could devote to the book before office hours began.

Enter Mary. Miss Mary to the clients, officially Mrs. James Allison. Last week a telegram had come from the Adjutant General's Office informing her with regret that her husband had been killed in action. She had been away from the office since then. Our poor useless words of comfort had already been said to her at her home; we could only smile at her as she entered. She was the gentle, tender one, worshipped by the clients, loved by us all. She felt of her desk, experimentally, as if for the first time; she walked to the file cabinet for case records, trying to teach herself that it all still existed exactly as before, though her husband was dead and life had stopped for her until she could accept his death.

Enter Miss Reeves, the girl without a first name. She signed herself M. Reeves. Surely she must have been conceived in passion; her creation must have taken nine months and, though none of us had evidence, she must have physiological habits like the rest of us. She smiled her fleeting, scared rabbit of a smile, hung up her shabby black coat and her shabby black hat and disappeared into her stall to be erased by her work, to become invisible by her duties.

Enter Elspeth Smith. Smitty. The career girl, the psychiatric caseworker, with experience in private agencies and hospitals, now doing a stint of generic casework in public welfare because she wanted her work history to include everything in the field. Her motto, we said to her face as well as behind her back, was Go to Freud, thou sluggard, and be wise. Her arms were heavy with editions of Menninger, Horney, and Adler. She now placed these along with the other books that lined her desk, then she blew on the weekend's accumulation of dust that had gathered on her collection of social work publications: *Survey Mid-Monthly*, *Survey Graphic*, and *The Family*.

Enter Gwendolyn Pierce. Gwen. The one we liked most, yet envied most because she made a prodigious amount of money writing confession stories. We didn't envy the hard work she did writing, just the large checks that came with her name on them. She was a success story: a poverty-stricken child who had worked her way through school, found the work she liked, and from it got material to write. Her charming and sumptuous house, furnished like every woman's dream, had been paid for, she said, by illicit love, juvenile delinquency, and illegitimate births.

Peg looked worried. "Where's Margy?" she said.

We glanced at Margy's empty desk, then at each other. The week before, the supervisor's bitterest censure had been for Margy and her lateness. Margy had spent tearful hours in the restroom recovering from Mrs. Patch's tongue; at her desk she had been listless and without hope. Peg and I moved to the window. As we looked down a battered car drove up; that would be Margy and her husband. We watched Margy get out of the car. Already her tasks had descended on her; even so far away we could see that she was groggy. Sleep hadn't rested her; she had jumped into the morning's demands, neglectful of the task she was doing because her mind was on the next job. Now she turned with a robot's gesture to get her husband's good-bye kiss, her mind already on the long day ahead at the agency and in her district. She rushed through the front door; after a while we heard the elevator jolt to a stop, steps raced up the hall, and Margy entered, wrestling to get her coat off, her blouse-tail hanging out of her skirt, her hair uncombed, and yet full of self-congratulation that somehow, in some way, she had got to work on time.

We waited for the grand entrance. It came. Mrs. Patch, our supervisor, entered. Bea had said once that her neck was Modigliani and the rest of her pure Neanderthal. None of us saw any reason to correct or to improve upon Bea's description. The politest names we called Mrs. Patch were hag, harpy, vixen. She entered as to a fanfare, as if she expected us either to stand at attention or to get down on our knees. She didn't say good morning; she looked at Peg's cigarette and ordered her to put it out. The rules were that we didn't smoke at our desks during office hours. Peg and I glanced at each other and our eyes said, but it's not eight thirty. Gwen looked at her watch. I picked up the telephone on my desk. The switchboard wasn't open and it had never been late in opening. I walked to the telephone on the clerk's desk which was left connected with outside. I dialed for the time. A flat, mechanical voice said eight twenty-four. The small triumph made me happy; then I was depressed, realizing that once again Mrs. Patch had reduced me to pettiness.

While I was making my infantile gesture of trying to prove Mrs. Patch wrong Peg had already put out her cigarette and was poking at an invalid geranium plant on her desk. She looked at it sadly and said: "On the bleakness of my lot, bloom I strove to raise."

Miss Reeves peered out of her stall; her tragic face lighted up in recognition and gratitude. "Emily Dickinson," she said.

Peg threw the flower pot into the wastebasket.

I thought again of each one in our division separately: Miss Reeves, the panic-stricken, the terror-stricken, doomed to quake before friend or foe or co-worker, the victim of wrath imagined or real; she found her refuge in poetry—those precious books set precisely on her desk, standing lean and thin: Shakespeare's sonnets and Donne's love poetry. Peg, the calm one, equal to any situation, good-looking; in college she had been voted the best all around, the president of the senior class, of student government; she had a quiet anger against the world for the heartsickness of too many of its people, for wars that ravage and for children crying for food; now she was waiting for her husband's return, her self divided by the necessary absence of her beloved, fighting in a war. Margy, the oldest one, tossed about by anxiety and insecurity, morbidly afraid of Mrs. Patch. Bea with her abiding love for painting and her equal love for people, her wild, erratic way of getting mixed up in everything, of being the innocent bystander who is dragged into all kinds of complications. And Gwen, well-dressed, finicky in her grooming, sweet-looking, every moment budgeted. Smitty, with her fine brain, the most intelligent one among us, her faculty of being impersonal; neat, but completely unadorned, no interest in clothes, yet with no hint of masculinity. And Mary, who was the symbol of love and unselfishness.

They all sat near me; we surrounded each other; each so different, yet each dedicated in her own way to social work, not all of us dedicated as Smitty was, as a lifelong profession, but we were conscientious about it: Margy until her young sons were educated; Peg until her husband came home from the army; the rest of us until love found us. Nowhere among us was the stereotype social worker: dowdy, stringy hair, flat-heeled Oxfords, mannish topcoat, a critical, didactic, unyielding attitude.

Then along with the others I settled down to work; the stalls were silent except for the whirring sounds made as we skimmed through the pages of the Budget Manual searching for figures to enter on the budget sheets, the quiet murmur of pencils, the faint crackling of forms as we bunched them together and inserted carbon paper.

At last Peg's voice jolted the quietness. In desperation she said: "Does anyone here have the slightest idea how much nine and seven are?"

"Sixteen," Smitty said. "If you'll just remember when you add nine to anything it's one less than if you were adding ten."

"That kind of information demoralizes me," Peg said. "Please keep it to yourself."

Hours passed. Ten thirty had come and no one moved. Usually we took ten or fifteen minutes off then for coffee or cokes. We became grimmer and grimmer. Mary borrowed a typewriter from the Stenographic Section and staggered in with it. She started typing at her desk.

Sometime after eleven Mary took an armful of case records to Mrs. Patch's office.

"Just a moment, if you don't mind." Mrs. Patch's voice struck us all. I saw Miss Reeves quiver; Peg shook her head in disbelief over Mrs. Patch's rudeness. I looked toward Mrs. Patch's office and saw Mary turn around and go back inside.

The screech that was Mrs. Patch's voice began again. "I've told you repeatedly that you are not to type records."

Harmony answered dissonance. Mary said in her clear, soft voice: "But I've been away for a week and Mrs. Carson is out today because her little girl is sick. They're days behind with the work. I thought—"

"The case records look bad enough without your wretched typing. When a stenographer is out the supervisor of the Stenographic Section can make arrangements for someone else to do the work. I will not have this repeated disregard for instructions and standard routine."

Mary stood in the door of Mrs. Patch's office, bludgeoned by the words that were shouted at her. I looked across at Peg; her face blazed in anger. Whatever the rules, she dragged out a cigarette and lit it. I took a pencil and punched at the calendar on my desk; soon the day was gouged out, only November and 1942 were left.

I shoved my chair back, grateful for the rasping sound it made, and walked toward Mrs. Patch's office. I tried to wait for her to finish a sentence, then saw there would be no end. I interrupted.

"I've a client to see at my desk."

Mrs. Patch's gross features reflected her pleasure in sadism; she almost smiled at me. "You haven't a client to see. You simply can't stand for Mrs. Allison to get criticism. None of you can take criticism."

"Mr. Ricks is waiting to see me," I said.

Mary went back to her stall and put her head on her desk. I had seen her like that when she was full of the sudden knowledge of her husband's death. I expected her to cry but after the sad week behind her she had no tears left; her body curved in the very shape of grief. I looked again at Mrs. Patch; her glare blotted me out.

At my desk I telephoned Mrs. Brown, the receptionist.

"Is Mr. Ricks in the waiting-room?"

"Save your breath for sensible questions," Mrs. Brown said. "You know he's here. He hasn't missed a day since the place opened."

"Send him up, please. Tell him I'll meet him at the elevator."

"Look, Jane."

"Yes."

"Before you hang up. Mrs. Logan was in a few minutes ago looking like death. I promised her you'd be out to see her some time today. She needs you. I know you're rushed with reviews but this is special."

"All right, Brownie, I'll go. It'll have to be after work."

Mrs. Patch's voice continued its shrieking.

"What's that?" Mrs. Brown said, hearing the shrieks over the telephone.

"The usual," I said. "Please tell Mr. Ricks to come up right away."

I went out into the hall to wait for him. The old cage elevator crept up with Mr. Ricks in it; his simian face peered out, his small, hungry, misshapen body followed his bent, protruding head.

"What you callin' me in for?" he said. "I ain't got no appointmint. I didn't ast to see you."

"You said the other day you needed some clothes."

"Yeah, but you said they closed out the clothing project and yall was gonna hafta be mighty partikler what clothes you give out from now on. How come you changed yore mind?"

Mr. Rick's cool and beautiful logic defeated me. He realized it and showed me no mercy.

"And you know as well as I do ain't no need to call me in to that desk of yourn if all you wanta do is write me up a order. You been writin' me up clothin' orders for three year and you know my size ain't changed none. I ain't lost a pound and I ain't growed a inch."

We were in the office then. He looked into each stall as we passed; his face twitched in disapproval at what he saw until we reached Mary. He stopped and looked at her in complete adoration; he placed her beyond the realm of womankind.

He sat down at my desk and I said: "How are you feeling today?"

"You know exakly how I'm feelin'. I got the most

ridiculous health in the world and you know it."

Mr. Ricks looked at me without confidence. He knew I was playing a lowdown trick of some kind and he resented it. I wanted to tell him that it was for his love, Mary, that I was doing it; perhaps he might have some pity for me if he knew that.

"Put me down for white shirts," he said. "I don't want none of them blue."

I pushed carbon in among the sheets of the clothing-order pad.

"You got two pieces of that stuff in one place and the other one is turnt wrong."

I thanked him. He watched while I placed the carbon correctly.

"Looka there," he said, "you left off the date. Ain't no dependence to be placed in women. Reckon I know. I had four wives and the Lord hisself couldn't keep count of what the Bible calls konkybines. Don't matter what they're doin' they gotta be watched."

I handed him a slip and told him to take it on down the hall to the clothing-room and get his shirts. He looked at the slip suspiciously and tucked it into his shirt pocket. He nodded his head as if he were on to my devil's work and left.

He banged the door shut. That was a signal for Smitty to dash out of her stall to the middle of the office.

"Now isn't that interesting?" she said. "Notice how he boasted about his well—masculinity. He's very unsure of it, so he boasts."

"Smitty," Peg said, "you're among friends. You can

use the right term for it. Potency. Virility. And you're right, but lots of people find out about those things. Word gets around. Even Freud is in the Modern Library, you know."

"Leave Mr. Ricks alone," I said. "I won't have him dissected. Get on back to your budget sheets."

Mrs. Patch's voice flooded over her door and landed at our feet, engulfing us in its tidal wave.

"This is not a college dormitory. It is not a woman's club. I will not have all that chattering."

"Nor, you poor hag," Peg said under her breath, "is it a woman's prison."

We shut our mouths, but our minds were nimble with unprintable thoughts about Mrs. Patch.

⊂⊃ ⊂⊃ ⊂⊃

I went alone to lunch at two, a rushed, gloomy affair at a counter with an eager little man breathing deeply down my neck, trying to budge me off the stool. He counted the forkfuls of food as I disposed of them; he was a coxswain urging me on to quicker endeavor. I wanted apple pie and shouted at the counter attendant when he made one of his oblivious runs past me. The man waiting behind me shook his head. In the mirror I saw him look scornfully at my hips. He seemed to place the apple pie on them. I would not be intimidated. I asked again modestly for the pie; once more the attendant ascended Olympus. And once more the little man won. As I got up my pocketbook deliberately opened itself and coughed up its contents. I went down to pick the junk up while the little man clambered over me to the seat, kicking me neatly in the jaw. His kind appears to be grown deliberately and especially for me.

The stalls were empty when I got back. I slipped a cylinder on the Dictaphone and dictated six home visits. I took the case records and the cylinders to the Stenographic Section. When I went back to the stalls I saw Smitty come out of Mrs. Patch's office. I hadn't seen Smitty's face like that, full of hate; her professionalism had left her, for the moment Freud was of no help. She didn't notice me as she walked past my stall to her desk.

I pulled my mail from the pigeonhole where it was stuck on the communal desk for messages and outgoing and incoming records and letters. Thumbtacked in the bulletin board over the desk was a notice in red underscored, announcing a staff meeting at four. There wouldn't be time to take care of the mail and requests sent up from the receptionist's desk, but I could sort them. I made separate piles of clothing-order requests, coal-order requests, visit requests.

Messages for other workers were mixed in with my mail, no unusual mistake, as sorting took a facility Miss Hawkins, the clerk, didn't have. Two were for Smitty. I hesitated to take them to her, not wanting to intrude on her anger. I went anyhow. She wasn't there. I placed the messages on her desk and looked at her scratch pad. Bea was the painter and artist

among us but Smitty had done well by the caricature
I saw: the flat nose and large mouth sketched on the
scratch pad belonged to no one but Mrs. Patch. The
rope around her throat and the distended eyes
and tongue showed that she had been hanged by her
neck until dead.

One of the messages was for Gwen. I took it to her
desk. Without halfway trying I saw a deposit slip for
eight hundred dollars. I looked at it enviously and
Gwen came in. I tried to pretend I hadn't seen the
checks and the deposit slip; I managed to knock them
all to the floor.

"I didn't mean to be nosy," I said.

Gwen said: "I don't mind at all. I'm proud of my
wages of sin." She looked at her watch. "Damn, it's
much later than I thought. The bank will be closed
so I can't make a deposit. I think I'll take the checks
downstairs and drop them in the mailbox."

I was alone again. A piece of paper accused me from
the spindle on my desk; I had written myself a message urging myself to write up a clothing order
for Tommy Green. He wanted some red pajamas; I
had underlined red. Tommy didn't want blue, he
wanted red. His mother had told me so, had screamed
it after me all the way up the street until I was out of
hearing.

I wrote the order and took it to the clothing-room.

Most of the clothes were gone since the clothing
project had been discontinued a short time before.
Work in the clothing-room was slack. Mrs. Sterling
and her assistant, Mamie, looked up from fan maga-

zines. They had been arranging Mamie's hair to match one of the covers. Mamie's mouth was lost in great curves of lipstick, her eyebrows had been replaced by two antler shaped lines that crawled steeply up her forehead.

Mrs. Sterling took the clothing order and handed me two pairs of blue pajamas.

"Tommy wants red," I told her.

"But we've only got four pairs of red. If you take some we'll have just two left."

"Red, please."

"Those people," Mrs. Sterling said. "They ought to be thankful for whatever color they can get. Living on charity."

"Red," I insisted. And then, improvising, I said: "Tommy's near death," and eased my conscience with the knowledge that he was near death in the house where he lived, near death because of the inadequate food he got and the dangerous places he had to play.

"Well, that's different," Mrs. Sterling said and immediately reached for the red pajamas.

All anyone had to do to please Mrs. Sterling and her kind was to die.

She made an extra flourish of the knot as she tied the bundle, as if this special fillip would in some way sustain Tommy.

"Poor little thing," she said. "I hope he gets better soon."

Mrs. Sterling and Mamie dismissed me.

"She's filing for a divorce," Mamie said. "Their careers don't mix. They don't have enough time to gether." Mamie talked about actresses as if they were confidantes who telephoned her long distance every night.

"I've got this cousin who went to Hollywood and she says—" Mamie whispered.

Whatever Mamie whisperered astounded Mrs. Sterling. "You don't say so," she said. "Well, I'll say, you'd sure never know it to look at her."

⊂⊐ ⊂⊐ ⊂⊐

At three thirty Bea said: "How about coffee?"

Everyone was in, staff meeting was only half an hour away. We stacked cases and letters and odds and ends as neatly as we could, anchored them down with paperweights and boxes of clips. We gathered around the coatrack, pulled coats from wire hangers that danced and clanged.

Miss Reeves said her usual: "I'm sorry but I can't go. I must finish these cases."

We got in the elevator, made a slow clanking descent to the first floor, and walked across the street to a joint. Bea somehow got caught in the middle of a traffic-light change; a truck driver shouted at her to get a seeing-eye dog. We walked ahead, then heard a scream from her, as she jabbed at water splashed all over her coat and stockings.

In the corner joint we shoved two tables together and dragged chairs around them.

Eddie, who owned the place, leaned across the counter and said: "What are you all giving away at the Relief today—G-strings?" He choked with delight over his wit.

We ordered coffee. Eddie shoved the cups toward us, floating in the saucers. The blue milk standing in a pitcher turned the coffee to a slate color when we poured it in; even in November three flies managed to claim the sugar bowl.

Eddie spoke to me as I handed the sugar to Margy. "I place bets with myself every day whether you'll take sugar. Sometime you do, sometime you don't."

Smitty glanced around at the dilapidated furniture, the flamboyant, flyspecked mural, the unmoving overhead fan with one broken blade like a snaggletooth, and said: "Eddie, do you practice hard or does it come naturally—the way you run this place?"

Eddie threw half-dry spoons in the center of the tables. "Takes years of practice," he said. "I have to work hard to keep this joint a joint."

Margy got change from Eddie and went to the telephone to make a call to see how her youngest son was. Smitty pulled out the current issue of *The Family* and started boning up on a review she was to give at the staff meeting. Margy pushed at the door of the telephone booth to try to get out. The door was stuck hard. We gathered around; in pantomime we gave suggestions to Margy.

Smitty said, "This place is like a Fun House, Eddie. You ought to charge admission."

"Really," Peg said, "George Price is the only one who could do justice to this joint."

"George Price," Bea said. "You mean Charles Addams."

Eddie knocked at the booth. "I don't see no way to get her out," he said. "Looks like we'll have to shoot her to put her out of her misery."

Margy gave one last terrific push and emerged.

We took our seats again around the tables.

"God, the places we go to every day," Margy said. This kind of talk was unusual for her; when she talked it was about her husband and her three little boys or about Mrs. Patch's persecution of her. "I tell myself I can't face another hungry child. Then I feel I can't face another hungry old person. I don't know which kind of case is hardest."

Smitty tossed *The Family* to an empty chair. "What kind of case really is hardest?" she asked. This was what she liked best, analyzing people, finding out what interested them, what repulsed them and why. "I suppose it depends on the kinds of persons we are."

Peg looked deeply into her coffee cup and said: "Well, for me adolescents are hardest. Those yens, those longings, that deadly job of trying to grow up. And the cases we have are even harder than the average adolescents because these kids go through all these things in broken homes, on relief, with no clothes and having no spending-money."

The talk excited us; we forgot Mrs. Patch, we forgot our own problems, we listened, yet our brains were partly busy with our own answers.

Bea said: "I believe it's the handicapped cases I find hardest. As long as you can walk and see and hear and speak, the world can be a wonderful place."

Smitty said: "It's the poor, frustrated women I'm sorriest for, waiting to love and be loved, to bear children."

Bea said: "Miss Smith, dear, don't be so personal."

Margy smiled and the smile erased the lines in her forehead, plowed there by worry over her family and clients and Mrs. Patch. We hadn't seen her smile for weeks. "If you little kiddies don't think that requited love has frustrations you're crazy."

Gwen whispered to Peg: "It's just like Smitty to drag sex in."

"You don't have to drag it in;" Smitty said. "It's always here. You ought to know, darling, you get paid so many cents a word for smearing it across paper and selling it to the confession magazines."

Mary had tried to be interested; she had worn a small, ineffectual smile to hide her grief; but now she showed genuine concern. "I'm sure it's the young children we ought to be worried about most. Each child is so new and precious, so young and trusting. And they can be molded so easily. And warped so easily."

Peg pushed her cup away; the spoon jangled against it. "The whole damned business is stupid—the whole assistance program. Imagine having to ask for help in a country as rich as this—going to an agency, making an application, having people ask you questions, going to your home, talking to your relatives."

Gwen tried to answer Peg; she went to the depths of her own harsh memories. "But I'm glad there is such a thing as our agency. If only there'd been one when I was a child. We were so poor, so desperately poor."

Gwen's remembered pain and humiliation shook us. At last Peg said: "Now, really, this talk is most unwomanly. Nobody is bitching about anything. Surely we can do better than this. I'd like to make a comment if I may. If I repeat myself, do forgive me. Mrs. Patch works harder and with more success at being a bastard than anybody I've ever known."

"You're entirely right," Gwen said.

Bea said: "Into every life some slut must fall."

"Watch them words," Eddie said, "they's gentlemen present."

The conversation broke up into small pieces. Smitty had gone back to the subject of sex and after a few remarks said to Gwen: "Well, if you think that, you've no idea what Freud meant by sex." Bea and Peg discussed the French poodles. In the last day or two Bill had developed a passion for hide-and-seek; Joe preferred walking on his hind legs. Bill liked jazz; Joe put up a howl if he couldn't have Schönberg. Margy and Mary talked about antiques, Margy's three sons, and recipes for Welsh rabbits.

Smitty looked at the clock that hadn't told time for months. "What happened to you, Eddie, at a quarter of seven that you had the clock stopped then?" she said.

"Aw, the damned thing ain't no good," Eddie said.

"It come with the place. I can't even give it away."

Margy looked at her watch and jumped up. "We've been here twenty minutes. Mrs. Patch will hold us up as awful examples at the staff meeting."

We got up, leaving the usual forlorn muck of saucers filled with cigarette stubs tinted with lipstick, cups stenciled with wavering red outlines of mouths.

We bolted and ran.

"Excuse me, ladies," Eddie shouted after us. "But that'll be seventy cents. Here we follow the old rule of asking our customers to pay."

Peg ran back through the rain and paid him.

"After this, to be on the safe side, I think I'd better count the spoons when you women leave," Eddie said.

He looked at us huddled under a small awning as we waited for Peg, and yelled: "It's a nice day for ducks." His guffaw filled the street. "Yes, sir, sure is a nice day for ducks and, my, how you all waddle." A new paroxysm of laughter seized him. "Be careful you don't lay too many eggs."

⊏⊐ ⊏⊐ ⊏⊐

WE PASSED by the waiting-room. Clients' voices rose at various pitches, filled with sorrow. Mary stopped to listen. Hands reached for her; the rest of us stood while the elevator made its slow descent to answer our buzz.

A woman grabbing at Mary said, "Miss Mary, they

taken my boy to jail. He run away. They got blood-hounds after him and found him. They tied him up and beat him till he died. They beat him till he died." Mary's voice was so low we couldn't hear her answer. The fatal beating had taken place thirty years before, yet it was born again each second in this poor woman's mind; weekly, sometimes daily, Mary comforted her.

Mr. Ricks, our watchdog, our self-appointed overseer, hunched against the wall. I nodded at him and he nodded back. He waved a bundle at me. "I got my shirts all right," he said. "That woman wanted to give me blue. I told her I watched you write up the order and your marked me down for white. That fixed her."

As we got in the elevator a man's voice followed us up the shaft. "I can't watch them little children starve to death. I just can't. I can't find no work. You all say I ain't due no relief bein' ablebodied. I'm gonna run off and leave them little children and then you all will have to do somethin'."

Mrs. Patch was patrolling the passageway between our stalls. Our behavior was beyond comment; she said nothing but made a hammy gesture of looking at her watch, shaking her head over our dereliction. She robbed us of what maturity we had; like naughty children we gathered up notebooks and scratch pads and pencils and went to the staff meeting.

The large room where we met was despairingly ugly with cracked plaster walls too long unpainted; unshaded bulbs swung from the ceiling; we sat on rickety cane-bottom chairs that squeaked at our slightest move.

Mrs. Patch and Mrs. Martin, the two senior supervisors of the main districts, sat in front facing us. They were at a large table that seesawed on uneven legs. Mrs. Patch blended with the ugliness of the setting; Mrs. Martin looked like the dear person that she was as she sat smiling at us.

The meeting followed a pattern; there were the usual reviews of articles in the current issue of *The Family*. The workers doing the reviews splattered them with enough professional terms so that there could be no mistaking that here was a gathering of social workers. We had to hand it to Smitty. She made her review stimulating when all we could do about the others was to thank God when they had finished. Someone from Intake made recommendations of new books in social work; a junior supervisor from the Children's Division presented two case histories. The senior supervisor of the Children's Division reported the alarming increase in juvenile delinquency since the beginning of the war. She shuffled some papers and said that during the year there had been an increase of thirty-eight per cent for boys over 1941; then she begged our pardon and said that was the increase in cases concerning girls and that the boys' increase had been seventeen per cent; she begged our pardon again and said she misread her own writing and that the increase for boys was eleven per cent.

After that there was quiet for a moment; then Mrs. Patch began her harangue. She did it with the relish of Burke and Hare viewing another dead body to cart off to Dr. Knox.

"Before I turn to some specific remarks and examples I'd like to say that I'm concerned about the things I overhear in the washroom and when you're in the halls. Sometime I wonder from your attitude and remarks whether you remember you're working as professional women or are simply making a collection of anecdotes about clients."

She settled her glasses halfway down her nose and gave the appearance of royalty visiting the scullery, prying in among the pots and pans and coming up with a dirty boiler.

"Now then, I'd like to read you some excerpts from case records." She pointed out some fine points in grammar. We were reminded that family is, not are; none is, not none are; data are, not data is. She flourished face-sheets improperly made out. She deplored errors in addition on budget sheets. She closed the case records and looked at the ceiling, as if we were really too much for her to settle her gaze upon. "You stay too long when you go out for coffee."

Peg dashed off a note. "The first time we've been out at all in more than a week. I knew she'd rave about it."

The censure continued. "Your desks are messy. Messier than any clerk's. I'd like to remind you that social work is a profession. You've standards to maintain, routines to follow meticulously, techniques to practice. All this sloppiness must be discontinued. I'm warning you for the last time." She piled all her notes together wearily. "I think that's all I have to say. Try to get back to work without the usual chatter and delay."

We dragged ourselves up.

Mrs. Martin smiled. "I'd like to say something, if I may." She nodded toward Mrs. Patch as if to get permission. The chairs squeaked as we sat down again.

Mrs. Martin's smile blessed us; her voice was a benevolence.

"Mrs. Patch said a great deal about records and record-keeping. You all know I'm an iconoclast. I don't want anything written down or kept in a record. I think we're presumptive when we try to keep records of anything as intricate as casework and human behavior."

In her quiet, gentle way she refuted Mrs. Patch; she congratulated us on doing work under almost impossible circumstances—the unbelievably rapid turnover in staff, the illness among those left, the heavy caseloads. As I listened to her words of encouragement my mind hunted for a metaphor or simile: her voice was a lullaby; no, a soft, gracious patting on the back for a job well done.

She was about to finish what she had to say. "And let's always keep looking at ourselves. Why do we do what we're doing? Why do we presume to think we can work with people? Let us search our own souls and go in the way of humility."

"Bless her," Margy whispered. "Heaven isn't going to be half good enough for her."

"That hag, that Patch," Bea said. "Reading from my recording. None can be either singular or plural except to a revolting purist."

We got up. I heard Mrs. Patch tell Mrs. Martin she wanted to talk to her privately at once.

We walked in lock steps toward the door. Somebody shouted: "Don't forget about the staff party tonight. Be sure to come. Gwen Pierce's house at nine."

We went back to work. The office was filled with the murmurs of pencils racing across forms; the November darkness hovered outside the windows; the rain poured down. With Mrs. Patch out of her office the place was almost cheerful.

The silence was dynamited; a shriek, a wail, a banshee cry rose from Miss Reeves's stall; obscenity rushed from her lips. Miss Reeves, the meek one, the rabbit, the Miss Milquetoast of the Social Service Bureau, who had never since recorded time spoken above a whisper, had turned into a woman of passion and anger.

"That devil Patch ought to die," she yelled. "Somebody ought to kill her." She ranted hysterically, her words meant nothing. She threw an ink bottle against the wall; it splattered like a vertical mud-puddle.

Peg wiped the ink smears from the partition and said calmly: "Come along, Miss Reeves, I'll take you home. It's long past quitting time." Peg handled Miss Reeves gently as if she were a little girl of four. She bundled Miss Reeves into her coat, pulled her hat down, poked the straggling hairs back, and took her by the hand.

They left, like an efficient nurse and an obedient catatonic patient.

The rest of us clustered in the passageway between the two rows of stalls, stunned by the miracle of Miss Reeves's raised voice. Gwen and Margy stood in wonder, inarticulate. All of Smitty's psychiatric terms left her; she said simply: "I'll be damned if I believe it."

Bea said: "It couldn't have happened. I don't care what anyone says, it's not possible that Miss Reeves could have talked like that."

There was silence while we all listened again to what our ears remembered. Miss Reeves's outburst sounded in them again. We hadn't said the words; we hadn't dared to say them. Yet the meekest of us had shouted what each of us felt.

C⅃ C⅃ C⅃

PEG and Miss Reeves had scarcely gone when Mrs. Patch came in, striding down our midst on her way to her office.

Margy grabbed her hat and coat, mumbling about groceries she had to buy on her way home. She said she would see us at the party later. Gwen, Smitty, and Bea bundled out after her in a welter of coats and galoshes and umbrellas.

I went to the rack for my coat. From the elevator came Smitty's voice. "I simply don't believe it," she kept saying.

Bea said: "All those beautiful, bawdy words. I had no idea Miss Reeves even knew they existed."

"Sweet Mother of God," Gwen said, "what would have happened if Patch had overheard?"

The elevator snapped shut on their other comments.

I longed to go home and rest before the party, but there was a visit I must make. I had promised Mrs. Logan I would see her.

My district lay close to the agency and I could walk to many parts of it. I decided to walk to Mrs. Logan's. I went past some of the small stores on Whitehall Street. In the window of one a pair of mice played, scampering up and down racks holding what cards described as Ladies' Choice Underwear. A bent, flimsy notice said in wavering letters, with upside-down n's, A Small Deposit Will Hold Any Article In This Window. The uneven sidewalk hoarded rain in small catchments.

In a little while I had left the stores and had come to the houses hid in darkness. Though it was the heart of a great city, oil lamps burned from some windows, not because the houses weren't wired but because kerosene was cheaper than electricity, and for the sometime sentimental reason that the soft, gentle light from lamps reminded people of homes in the country, left behind because the land gave no living or because the city had promised so much.

I turned into Central Avenue and in a moment the great hulk of a dark house was before me. My feet stumbled along the ridges of loose bricks leading to the

house; I walked up the splintery steps to a porch floor
that quaked beneath me. I stopped in the hall, not
daring to begin the treacherous ascent of the stairs.
I called to Mrs. Logan.

Above me a door opened.

"Do be careful," Mrs. Logan said. "Those stairs are
dangerous."

A trickle of light from her room swept down the
stairway. She brought a candle and helped me like a
guide who knows precisely where mountain crevasses
must be crossed.

"Be careful of the third step, try to skip over it,
there's no tread."

Upstairs she pulled me toward a corner of her room.
We cowered there as if we were plotting some great
betrayal. Except for the table at which we sat, the furniture didn't show. The light bulb had been swaddled
in newspaper so that one beam fell in a minute circle
to the floor. A lump of humanity lay on the bed. Every
now and then a whimper, like a small hurt puppy's,
came from it. I didn't look into Mrs. Logan's eyes;
I had looked too often into them. She was past suffering and endurance, her body was impaled on the
jagged spears of waiting. Her voice began an almost
monotonous chant, each word familiar to her tongue,
each word infected with despair and hopelessness.

"I ask myself a dozen times an hour, how long can
he live? Why doesn't he die? It's been like this now
for six years, sitting with him day after day and
night after night. Never anyone to help me. I call all
the hospitals. I use different voices. They're all used

to my own voice by now after all these years. I say to
them, something has got to be done. You must take
him. I can't look after him any longer. And they say
they're sorry but they can't take chronic cases. The
city doctor comes, the Grady doctor comes and they
say they can't understand how he can live.

"I sit here trying to remember how he used to save
so that I could have a pretty hat or we could take
a special trip. I think of the way he remembered
birthdays and anniversaries and Valentine, anything
as an excuse to give me a present. I remember how
dear he was to Mama during her last illness. I remember his kindness to everyone, to all the children
on the street—running errands for sick people and old
ones. I look at him, all his goodness has come to this,
to a whimper, to something less than a baby.

"Time after time I run away. I leave. I say I won't
come back. I'll go to another town. I'll get a job. I'll
take another name. I'll forget him lying here. I find
myself at the station. I get to the ticket window. I'm
the next one in line. Then I'm there. The man is looking at me saying where to lady and I name a place
far away, knowing I haven't the money to pay for
the ticket, knowing I'll run back here before the
man has had time to stamp the ticket.

"Sometime I think I'll kill him and me. Death must
be sweet and good after all this. My life is nothing
but sitting and waiting and shuddering at his whimpering and lifting him and trying to feed him and make
him comfortable. And I can remember going to movies
and caring what the neighbors said and thinking I

was lucky because I was married to him. I remember planning when we could own a house."

Mrs. Logan made cups of her hands to catch her tears. "My God, I can remember being anxious about whether a cake I was baking might fall.

"I curse the time I looked at him, curse whatever fate or chance brought us together. Today I almost did it. I thought, God, let them hang me, anything, I can't stand it any longer. Then I decided I'd kill us both. And while I was putting some clothes away, tidying up the place so whoever found us wouldn't find too much of a mess—my dear, it might have been you finding us at this moment—I came across a note he had written years ago. 'Thank you, my darling, for loving me.' That's what he had written. 'Thank you, my darling, for loving me.' "

From the bed Mr. Logan's whimpering started again and increased to a wail.

There was nothing I could say or do. Mrs. Logan knew that.

Our eyes entered into a conspiracy of wishing death for her husband soon.

Then we said good night.

⊂⊐ ⊂⊐ ⊂⊐

A CROWD stood limply waiting for the Decatur car. I saw faces tired from the day's demands, bodies impatient for home and food, favorite radio programs, whatever mail had come, the dozens of details that would end the day. The car came. We jockeyed for places where we thought it would stop, it overshot our mark, we jostled and shoved toward the door. I climbed on assisted by the jabs and pushes of the man behind me, detained by the hulk of a woman's body just ahead.

We rode out Auburn Avenue, past stores, the offices of the *Daily World*, banks, insurance offices, churches, The Golden Rod Tavern, The Too Tight Barber Shop, pressing clubs; then on to Edgewood Avenue and more small stores, past rooming-houses, one-family houses; a sharp turn to the right at Hurt Street, then on to DeKalb, houses lining the narrow, crowded street on the left, on the right railroad tracks paralleling the streetcar tracks. The car made stops as the buzzer sounded, its door banged open, the conductor pulled a cord, two bells rang, we started again, grinding and swaying to our destinations. I squinted at the night through the rain-blurred windows; I found a landmark; it was time for me to get off. I teetered down the crowded aisle, made a long reach toward the conductor, across heads, to hand him my transfer and got off at the stop beyond Kirkwood.

I walked a block to where I lived.

Upstairs I didn't turn on the lights in my living-room but went straight to the kitchen. The refrigerator yielded up two shriveled carrots, half a bottle of milk, and some satiny, tasteless processed cheese. I got it all down without too much trouble, along with a lecture to myself that this was no way to eat; I made resolutions about balanced meals in the future—meat, vegetables, a salad. Then I began to tidy up. The milk bottle was stubborn about coming clean. I scrubbed at the hardened white ring in the middle and got my eyes splashed with suds. I washed the disconsolate breakfast-dishes, telling myself that I must find time to wash them every morning before I left. I washed the dishcloth, swept the kitchen floor, and watered the pots of philodendron.

I turned on the lamps and lay down for a moment in the living-room, liking the way it looked since Peg had helped me with it, remembering the stiff necks we had for a week after painting the ceiling, the stiff backs after painting the walls and floors. I loved the room. The walls were dead white, the floor covered in a deep red carpet, the couch cover a bright rich blue. My pride was a large chest Peg had done in yellow, red, black, and blue, with some tricky treatment in varnish to make it look very old. In wooden frames over this chest were grouped children's portraits from various centuries and places: Lady Jean, The Girl With Watering Can, Madame Vigée-Lebrun's portrait of her little girl peering into a mirror, a bright-eyed stoic New England boy done by some unknown painter, a girl child painted by Mary Cassatt, Goya's little boy in red holding to a pet crow on a string—that appealing child with the formidable name of Don Manuel Osorio de Zuniga. Bea had made the frames; she insisted that no group of children's portraits could be really pleasing without Manet's Lina Campineanu. Somewhere she found a print and added that wistful little girl to the collection. There was a fireplace that drew without wheezes, its mantel unadorned except for a decanter and three sherry glasses. I lay there enumerating my treasures, trying not to think of Mrs. Logan and her husband who was splayed upon his bed as if on a medieval rack.

Then I glanced fondly, with avarice even, at the wall covered with shelves holding my collection of murder stories, mystery stories, detective stories, supernatural stories, accounts of murder trials, studies of real murders. I thought of their writers' names and the names made poetry and music in my mind: Edmund Pearson, Dorothy L. Sayers, Oliver Onions, Ellery Queen, Wilkie Collins, H. C. Bailey, Margery Allingham, Mrs. Belloc Lowndes, Joseph Shearing, Agatha Christie, William Roughead, Elizabeth Daly, Graham Greene, Eric Ambler, Ngaio Marsh, Michael Innes, Dashiell Hammett, Raymond Chandler, F. W. Crofts, Nicholas Blake, and all the others whose works I had only to reach out to touch. I pulled out *Strong Poison* and found the place where the memorable first meeting of Harriet Vane and Lord Peter occurs, in prison, Harriet on trial for her life. My eyes ate up the familiar words: "Good afternoon, Miss Vane," and her answer: "Please sit down."

There was a knock at the door. Still enchanted by Harriet Vane and Lord Peter, I said: "Come in."

Peg entered, lovely in a long green taffeta skirt and chartreuse blouse.

I slipped *Strong Poison* back in its place. Peg didn't care at all for detective stories.

"I came early," she said. "We might try to get there before the others. Gwen may need help."

She surprised me by not saying anything about the book I had held; she usually had a tidy diatribe to deliver about people who wasted time reading murder novels.

"Let's have some sherry," I said. "Then I'll bathe."

I took the decanter and two glasses from the mantel.

Peg sat on the couch. I slumped in a chair. I wanted to speak of my misery over Mrs. Logan, over things generally, but I couldn't; Peg seemed to have brought sadness too. She looked hard at me. I pretended to be fascinated by the sherry glass, turning it in my hand, watching its facets pick up flickers of light from the lamp near by. Suddenly pain shook Peg. "I didn't get a letter from Mark today—that makes six weeks since I've heard. He may be dead."

I started weeping for Peg, for Mrs. Logan, for Mary, for everyone. "How can you say such a thing?" I said.

"Why not? If it doesn't happen to Mark it's happened to thousands of men and will happen to thousands more? Who am I to be the lucky one? Mary wasn't lucky."

Peg fumbled in her cigarette pack and found it empty. She said something mildly obscene and I tossed my pack to her.

I said: "I went to see Mrs. Logan tonight."

Peg shook her head. "I had the case once. Mr. Logan lies there day after day. His wife sits there with him. They lead dead lives."

"Isn't there some way we could let someone know about this suffering—all this needless waste of human beings?"

Peg laughed an unpleasant laugh. "The human race hasn't time for pity. What can you do? What can I do? Look what Hogarth did. Look what Blake wrote. Think of *The Song of the Shirt*. But before all of them there was the simple statement, feed my sheep. What can we do when no one has paid any attention to their genius? How many people are in anguish at this very moment? Just try to think if you can of the indifference of the sane. Most of us say so long as it isn't my child who is hungry or my lover who isn't killed, it's all right. And here you and I sit and talk and smoke and sip sherry ever so daintily. We ought to be frightened out of our wits at our composure. The people who terrify me are those who don't become alcoholics and who don't end up in madhouses."

She poured more sherry for us and began to speak quietly. "We know so much. We know slums breed juvenile delinquents. Slums breed disease. Not every child in a slum is a juvenile delinquent. Not every person in a slum is diseased. But the odds are too much against them. We're putrid with research projects and statistics and norms and means but nobody really does anything—well, a little maybe, but pathetically little."

Peg stopped talking. After a while she said: "Why don't you go take a bath?"

I did as I was told. In my small bathtub I doubled up like a fetus.

I heard Peg at the bookshelves reading titles:

"*Studies in Murder, Five Murders, Instigation of the Devil, The Evil Men Do, Twelve Scots Trials, Malice Domestic, Bad Companions, The Life and Times of the Detective Story, The Red Arrow Mystery, The Murder of Roger Ackroyd, The High Window, Who Killed Aunt Maggie, The Golden Violet, The Strange Case of Lucile Clery, Artists in Crime.* Good heaven, don't you have anything but this stuff?"

That was an old familiar question. It was coming after all, the old familiar argument.

"Many intelligent people like murder stories," I said.

"Please don't quote Philip Guedalla about the reading of detective fiction being the relaxation of noble minds."

We had had this discussion so often that she was picking up my lines.

"Some of the finest writing ever done has been in mysteries—even your precious Henry James tried them."

"*The Turn of the Screw* is not a murder story."

"It's placed among mysteries—how else would I know about it?" I climbed into my dress. "Anyway, please shut up about detective novels and come help with these buttons." She did as I asked.

"Nice," she said, looking at me when I had finished dressing.

"Thank you," I said. "Nice is such an overwhelming compliment."

"It's all I'm up to."

Outside on the street we had no success to speak of

in jumping puddles. At last we reached Peg's car; as it moved along the rain-peppered street she began to tell me about Miss Reeves.

"When I think of that poor soul—the life she leads between those two women, Patch and her mother. Her existence is haunted. The poor darling was in a state of collapse when we got to her house, but her mother wouldn't take a moment of having any attention paid to anyone but herself. She stood around whining about all the sacrifices she had made for her daughter; she grabbed at her heart and screamed from imaginary pain. She went into a temper tantrum that would have made a two-year-old envious. That poor Miss Reeves lives in a rat-race between the office and home. She cooks for her mother. She sits with her. She's waked up during the night by her. Her evenings are full of the suffering Mrs. Reeves has undergone during the day when she has been left all alone without a soul to turn to. By the way, Miss Reeves's name is Matilda. Pretty, isn't it? Of course her mother has botched it into Mattie. After spending the early morning getting her dear mother in shape to meet the day's crises Miss Reeves comes to the agency to be supervised by Patch. I don't know how she's taken it all these years. Maybe today's outburst will save her. Do you know what that Patch did? She withheld a raise from Miss Reeves for six months. Naturally the mouse wouldn't have nerve enough to ask for it; after all, we're supposed to get raises without asking for them. Finally she wrote a note and Patch wrote a note back saying she was incompetent and a raise couldn't be recommended for her. If any of us does a good job it's Miss Reeves. Everyone knows it. Even Miss Reeves suspects it. Which is why somehow or other she got up enough nerve to pitch a nice fit."

We rode for a long time, then Peg said: "Mr. Reeves is dead. Of drink." Her voice took on a querulous tone; she became Mrs. Reeves talking to Miss Reeves. "If only your good-for-nothing father hadn't died and left us, things would have been different. He spent his last penny on drink." Peg was Peg again.

"That dear Mr. Reeves lying in the gutter dead must have known how lucky he was to escape."

By that time we were far out on Peachtree Road. Soon we stopped in front of Gwen's house, in Georgian style, beautiful and stately, though not very large, far back from the street, its great lawn encircled by boxwood.

Peg said, in reference to nothing we had mentioned: "Damn sublimation. Damn being without my husband. I'm so tired of all this chastity."

What she said didn't require any answer, but to show her I was in a friendly, responsive mood I said: "Aren't we all?"

╒╕   ╒╕   ╒╕

GWEN greeted us in a blue velvet dress over which she wore a white pinafore embroidered in peasant designs. We walked from room to room exclaiming over the antiques, the Coromandel screen, the

Sèvres china; the house was a joy, done with taste that hid lavishness. Fires burned in the living-room and the dining-room and the library. I remembered what Gwen had said earlier in the day about the wages of sin. All this was bought with stories of abortions, illegitimate births, illicit loves. In a corner of the library on a small desk sat the typewriter that ground out the stories; near it lay a neat stack of white paper.

Peg asked if she could help. Gwen mentioned something about coffee and they went to the kitchen, a room that showed itself behind the swinging doors as a colorful, inviting place, not one of those gleaming white affairs which make getting a meal seem like doing a piece of surgery.

Workers from the agency began to come; three from the Children's Division, two from Intake, then a great surge from Intake, four from Mrs. Martin's division. Mrs. Martin wasn't coming—she had a sick child to look after; we didn't expect Miss Reeves and Mary. Out of the staff of seventy fully sixty must have come. We said hello brightly to each other and admired clothes and hair-dos. There was much drifting in and out of the luxurious rooms, pawing of books, peering at pictures, squealed greetings, much cooing as if we hadn't all been in each other's hair days without end. As usual, cliques of friends clustered together, ignoring, except for the briefest wave or hello, everyone else. There were games nobody played with enthusiasm and music everybody talked above and not very good coffee and very weak tea; the usual agony of a party no one wanted to come to in the first place and yet everyone was drawn to by the nauseating pull of obligation. To prove that it was a gathering of professional social workers, every now and then there would wing its way above the gossip and war talk the mention of Gordon Hamilton or Viola Paradise or Fern Lowry or Dr. Ogburn or Dr. Odum. A classicist among us even mentioned Mary Richmond, the mother of us all.

Mrs. Patch came late; her appearance was all that was needed to make the party a complete flop. Conversations started only to dwindle into monosyllables. Involved questions were asked and got simple yeses and noes for answers; more often mere nods or shakes of the head.

After an incalculable time of silence someone from the Children's Division said, seeing that rock bottom had been reached: "Smitty, you've simply got to do the psychiatric caseworker talking to the madam of a house who has been mistaken for a foster mother."

From somewhere there was an unenthusiastic: "Please, Smitty."

Smitty needed no urging.

Someone from Intake rushed for the john. "I can't take it, not another word of it," she said. "I'm going to turn on the water as hard as it will turn on so I can't hear it. Somebody please come get me as soon as Smitty finishes."

There were a few titters as Smitty made herself into a so-called typical social worker. She twisted her stocking seams, let her stockings sag, drew her hair back tight, tucked her dress up so that her slip showed, and began her skit.

We were stretched on a rack of synthetic hilarity.

Halfway through Smitty's piece there was a scratching at the door. Mrs. Patch's sister-in-law, Miss Ellen Fitzgerald, trembled at the entrance, a slender, wispy bundle of anxiety.

"I knocked but no one heard me." She whispered so that only those nearest her could hear. "So I came on in—I thought—well, Jennifer, you told me to be here exactly at ten thirty—exactly, you said, so—"

Mrs. Patch said: "For heaven's sake, Ellen, come on in. And speak up."

Gwen held out her hand. "It's so good to see you. Please come in."

Smitty had been caught midway in one of her gestures. In defeat she said: "Oh, well, you've heard it dozens of times. You know how it ends." She began to straighten her stocking seams.

"Did I interrupt—I'm so sorry. I—I—" Miss Fitzpatrick stood as erectly as she ever did but she might have been groveling on the floor.

Gwen said: "Please come along to the dining-room."

Miss Fitzpatrick followed her as if she were being led by a jailer.

"Will you have tea or coffee?" Gwen asked.

Miss Fitzpatrick looked in dismay at the silver pots. "I really don't know—I—well, I really like them both —but it's rather late and I wouldn't like to be kept awake—still—"

The rasp of Mrs. Patch's voice filled the room. "Don't act like an idiot, Ellen. Say what you want."

"Tea," Miss Fitzpatrick said. "I mean—coffee, if you don't mind."

Peg poured from one of the pots and handed a cup to Miss Fitzpatrick.

"Thank you, my dear. Thank you so very much," she said and looked at the coffee as if it were hemlock. The cup leaped from the saucer as her unsteady hands grasped for it.

Coffee spilled on the satin cover of a chair and on the rug.

Gwen screeched; then looked in horror at Miss Fitzpatrick.

"I'm so sorry, so terribly sorry," Miss Fitzpatrick said. "I've ruined it. I mean, I've ruined them—your beautiful chair and your lovely rug." She began to cry.

Gwen recovered. "But it's quite all right," she said. "It doesn't matter at all. I know exactly how to get the coffee out. It's happened a number of times. Please don't think anything about it."

Miss Fitzpatrick backed into a chair and fell in it. She burrowed her nose into a handkerchief. "I'm so sorry, so very sorry. I'm so clumsy—I—"

Peg hurried to get another cup of coffee.

"Really," Miss Fitzpatrick said, "don't give me another. I'd only drop it, too. Look at my hands. They tremble so. I've no control."

"Stop talking like a fool," Mrs. Patch said, enjoying Miss Fitzpatrick's agony; the familiar glint of sadism was in her eyes.

Peg ignored Mrs. Patch. "Then I'll hold it for you.

You've had a long cold drive and you need something hot." She stood over Miss Fitzpatrick and held the cup. Miss Fitzpatrick lapped with the abject humility of a beaten dog.

The clock struck eleven. The curse and the enchantment ended, we could go home. Guests began to leave one by one as if to secret and important destinations, lying in their teeth about the most marvelous time and the most marvelous staff party we'd ever had. At the door their good-byes were snatched by a fierce wind and sent to oblivion.

Peg and Margy and I stayed to help Gwen clean up. We made small sorties about the rooms, emptying ashtrays, straightening bric-a-brac, rearranging chairs, sliding records back in cabinets.

Peg assumed the martyr's role of dishwasher. With a stack of dishes climbing from her hands up past her shoulders, she stopped in the kitchen doorway and said a few words of billingsgate to Gwen about her treatment of Miss Fitzpatrick.

"I acted a shrew and I know it," Gwen said. "I'm sorry. Poor, terrified Miss Fitzpatrick. My look was murderous when she spilled the coffee. I've told you before—you don't really get over deprivations. At least I'm afraid I never will. Tonight when the chair and rug were stained I was a small child being done out of something. I've had these lovely things a long time now, but I can't take them for granted. When any of them is scratched or spoiled I get in a rage."

Peg got a boiling kettle of water and a bottle or two from a cleaning closet. She worked at the stains. "I don't give a damn about your precious furniture," Peg said. "What I'm worried about is Miss Fitzpatrick. That fiendish Patch has destroyed her soul."

Suddenly, very suddenly an overwhelming wish to get out of that beautiful house came to me. I wanted to leave the place where spilled coffee or a stained rug took precedence over a human being, I wanted to shut the door on the room where Miss Fitzpatrick's dignity had been stripped from her, first by Mrs. Patch and then, though less unkindly, by Gwen.

"I want some air," I said. "I'll be waiting for you outside, Peg."

The rain had quieted to a mist; the mist made halos around the street lights; the grass licked damply at my feet; I pulled at a limb of a tree and a private shower of rain fell around me.

"My God," a voice said, "is that how you commune with nature?"

Someone leaned out from a parked car. It was Ted, Margy's husband. I felt indignant, my privacy had been invaded. I felt as I used to feel when my brother snatched a note from my beau out of my hand. I was polite but very aloof; I said hello to Ted and nothing else.

"Where're the others?"

"They'll be here in a minute."

"I want to talk to you, Jane. I've been wanting to talk to you for weeks. It's about Margy. Something's got to be done. It's as if she's gone away and left me and the boys all alone. She isn't herself. Her mind isn't on anything. She mutters. She doesn't even do things half-heartedly, she doesn't do things at all. She cries. She talks to herself—you know about who, of course— that woman Patch."

"Mrs. Patch affects us all that way."

"Not the way I'm talking about. She couldn't possibly."

I told him what had happened to Miss Fitzpatrick a few moments before.

Ted said some words he had picked up from his younger brothers in the army. "Would that woman— would Mrs. Patch talk to me? Could I tell her what she's doing to Margy?"

"I don't think it would do any good."

I was glad I couldn't see Ted's face, his voice had hell's agony in it.

"I want to try. I've got to talk to her. I don't want Margy to know anything about it, though."

"Why don't you come some night? Mrs. Patch usually works until seven or eight." I told him how he could come in the back way, how he'd know Mrs. Patch was there by the light in her office.

Peg and Margy came out. Ted whispered: "Please don't mention this."

There were the usual prolonged good-nights, thoughts of no importance had to be shouted as if the world's destiny depended upon them, there was scurrying back for a dropped handkerchief, a forgotten pack of cigarettes. Finally we left with Gwen still shouting something about we were please to forgive her for being a shrew to Miss Fitzpatrick.

Peg and I had nothing to say to each other on the

way home. She let me out and I closed the car door. I thought I heard her say something. I opened the door and asked her what she had said. "I hadn't expected to say it aloud, but since you heard me I will. It's brutal, I know, brutal beyond belief, but what Miss Reeves said this afternoon is right. Mrs. Patch shouldn't live."

I watched Peg's car turn the corner. I stood for a long time trying not to think of what she had said. I ran up the stairs.

In my rooms as I performed the ceremony of throat creaming, hair brushing, window raising, putting an extra blanket at the foot of the couch in case it turned colder, I thought of the sad day: Mary's grief, her return to the office, the lie I told to try to protect her from Mrs. Patch's tongue; the lie I told to get red pajamas for Tommy Green; the sketch Smitty had made of Mrs. Patch hanging dead; Miss Reeves's outburst; the visit to Mrs. Logan; the useless agony of the party; Miss Fitzpatrick's humiliation; Ted's misery over Margy.

The thoughts circled around in my brain like a merry-go-round circling to funereal music, with no gay ponies, no brightly painted chariots, but black horses pulling a hearse. Sleep was far from me. The merry-go-round moved slower and slower to sadder and sadder music.

And then my eager fingers reached for *101 Years' Entertainment*, a collection of murder stories. They turned quickly and surely to *The Hands of Mr. Otter-mole.*

My brain stopped its sad, futile meanderings and focused on Mr. Whybrow, trudging home from work, on his way to be murdered. Be wary, Mr. Whybrow, my excited mind warned, escape the hands of Mr. Ottermole, dart down some alley, escape, escape. Yet I knew there was no escape and Mr. Whybrow would continue on in his accustomed way; instead of his home and tea, death and murder waited for him; they would snatch him from all familiar things into darkness and terror and the grave's deep forgetfulness.

THE rain beating against the windows waked me. Soon the alarm went off, the signal for early morning tortures to begin. That fraud between seven and eight which calls itself an hour was upon me; it was there racing the clock, snipping minutes. I acted under self-hypnosis, counted out tablespoons of coffee, got out the toaster, blew the accumulation of crumbs from it, padded to the bathroom and rushed water into the tub. With an unsteady hand I scooped up the paper from the hall. I read the headlines and Ralph McGill's column, then took a shallow dip into the bathtub. The coffee was ready then. Toast took only a moment but not quite as long a moment as I gave it. I scraped the pieces and spread them thinly with butter. I went in then for a great deal of bustling carried out under the anæsthesia of half-sleep, sweeping a spot in the middle of the rug, emptying ashtrays, making up the studio couch, running water over the dirty dishes, dumping a mound of used coffeegrounds on an old newspaper.

Lipstick did passably well on the left side, but wavered surrealistically on the right. I had another go at it while the clock leaped to eight ten.

I missed the streetcar; my one special talent was for missing streetcars. A cluster of people gathered with me at the car stop. There was the phony cordiality of early morning greetings, the stale complaints about the rain. Another car came, jammed. We all climbed on, pushing, molding ourselves like dough in biscuit tins.

The night before I had left a Visiting sign on my desk, so I didn't go to the agency but went directly to my district. At Pryor and Edgewood I transferred to a Washington-Lakewood car. At Rawson Street I got off in the rain and walked.

I passed the bleak, dank houses with their sagging porches and their tumbled-down steps. Once rich people had lived here, leaving as evidence sweeping staircases and mirrored walls and colored glass windows and clothes closets ·big enough for bedrooms now. The rich had moved on and the poor had moved in. The slender tide of the rich flowed on, and their large places that housed at most eight or ten had been so overwhelmed by the surges of the poor that forty or fifty lived where ten had lived before. These houses that had been filled with laughter and plenty now housed poverty that strips naked and hunger that demoralizes minds and souls. Their inhabitants were debased by the fear of no next meal and no lodging unless money for the next week's rent could be miraculously found; lives lived in the negation of need and want. And all around, pellagra, anemia, malnutrition were creeping in, not rapidly with quick welcomed death, but with endless slowness, nibbling away at self-respect and hope and all of energy except the minimum needed for the barest subsistence.

I thought of the differences in the appearance of these houses from summer to winter. In hot weather the residents spilled out on the brief front yards, overflowed into the streets. Winter pulled them back into the broken shelters, to make the closest half-circle possible around the grate, warming the fire as much as they were warmed by it, fires so faint their smoke hardly reached the chimneytops.

I stopped at the first house on my list of visits.

Mr. Jones came to the door, his eyes closed equally with sleep and suspicion. I told him why I was there, that it was time to review his grant. He moved from the door.

"Well, come on in if you gotta. I just don't know how a one of you all has got the right to be nosin' in and out of my business astin' questions. You all are on the Relief the same as us. If it wasn't for the likes of us there wouldn't be the likes of you, so don't give yoreself no airs."

We went to the kitchen and sat near an oil stove; one wick blinked. "I don't build up a fire till towards evenin'. Ain't no sense wastin' coal. Warm myself here of a mornin' while I do what little cookin' I'm able to do."

We talked. Poverty had corroded his body. His will had been broken by rejections and refusals; still his great spirit showed in every word he said. "I want work the same as any other man. But they say to me, what we want with a old man like you ain't got a tooth in yore head when we got young high school graderates can do twict the amount of work you can. And here when I'm forced to crawl on my hands and knees and belly to ast you all for a little somethin' to keep me from perishin' you keep checkin' up on me. Miz Ruzvelt would bawl her eyes out if she knowed how you all was carryin' on up there. Now I got somethin' else on my tail. The Grady is actin' just as high assed as you all, sayin' I oughta have my tonsils took out, was poisonin' my system and I says to them if the Lord aimed for me to go without tonsils he'd a not give me none to start with and whatever you say I ain't a goin' over there and be cut on by no interne. Them young fellers turnt loose over there with knives ain't got gumption enough to slice a piece of ham."

After a while we took leave of each other and I walked to the next house.

Mrs. Watkins was happy to have me, happy to have anything that broke the monotony of her day.

"Here, take a rocker," she said. "It's mighty nice to have company."

We settled down in rockingchairs before the two-eyed heater that doubled as Mrs. Watkins's cookstove and listened to what each other had to say.

"Joe and me we just set here all the time, nothin' to do. Lord, on the farm you don't set much. I set here recollectin'. We done things, always was twict as much for yore hands to do as you had time to do 'em. All of us taken a hand in plantin', men folks plowed, us women folks and girls hepped hoe, done our share of choppin' cotton. We watched and waited. Was mighty afeared at times. Weather meant somethin' to us then, not like now when it means just to put on yore coat or to carry a umbreller. Now our eatin'— what little they is of it—comes out of a paper poke. Then every mouthful except for the sugar and coffee and salt was growed right there on the place. Here in town ain't nothin' to watch grow, no corn ner cotton ner biddies. Nothin' to take on over ner to worry about. I tell Joe we just set here like sacks of salt. I tell Joe looks like the Lord turnt us into sacks of salt, like he was mad with us same as he was with Lot's wife. Rest ain't precious no more. I can remember the little bit of rest I'd git drinkin' a cold drink of water fresh drawed from the well, lookin' out acrost the fields, sometimes restin' rockin' on the porch a minute or two but hands always full of somethin', crochetin' or darnin'. Nothin' like none of that now. No settin' up with the sick. Here they just haul 'em off to the Grady. I think and study about things a lot. Don't have nothin' else to do. We loved our childern and done the best we knowed how for 'em. I love Joe. He's a mighty good man, worked hard all his life. Yes, ma'am, as I say, I love Joe and I love the children and the grandchildern and I guess they's lots of kinds

of love but settin' here studyin' it come over me ain't
no love like the love a woman has for a cow and a
man has for a horse."

We rocked on for a few minutes, the room silent except for the rockers hitting the floor and the bubbling
sound of the kettle of water boiling on the heater.
Then we worked out her budget and I told her I had
to go. She said they had a nice mess of greens and
would be proud if I'd come back for dinner. I thanked
her and said good-bye.

On the next visit Mrs. Smith rushed me, as if she
were expecting someone and she didn't want whoever her guest was to know she got public assistance.
Many clients were embarrassed when people dropped
in on them while the social worker who had their
case was with them. At various times I had been intro-
duced as a cousin, a neighbor, a missionary, a school-
teacher, a nurse, an insurance collector. I finished as
quickly as I could.

I barely got to the street when Mrs. Smith bounded
after me, pulling a frayed coat around her shoulders.
"I been dyin' to ast you somethin' ever since you
come," she said. She stood in front of me and grabbed
my elbows as if to make sure I couldn't escape.
"Honey, I didn't get up the gall to ast you inside but I
guess I've got the face to ast you here. I ast Miz
White and I ast Miz Sims, seein' as how they're as
good a neighbor both of them as I've got and as a
body could want. They said they never heared
nothin' like it and they said if they was me they'd ast
the vizter."

She pulled me toward her and whispered something quite interesting in my ear.

"Yes, ma'am, honey, every single time he does. Now, have you ever heared of anythin' like that? Don't it take the cake? Don't it beat the band? Have you ever heared anythin' to equal it?"

I remembered several summers before on a deadly hot afternoon everyone at summer school had dozed during the long hours of a technical lecture. The psychiatrist conducting the seminar said, possibly to wake us, possibly to shock us: "I want you to realize that there's nothing about sex that is perverted; variations yes, but perversions, no." I was about to reassure Mrs. Smith with the psychiatrist's wisdom; then I realized it would be discourteous, because when prodigious things happen to you, you don't want to hear someone say they are quite ordinary. I looked at Mrs. Smith with congratulation and awe and told her I'd never in all my life heard of such a thing.

Mrs. Adams was in her kitchen, ironing. She had no ironing board and used the kitchen table, teetering on uneven legs, shifting from one leg to the other as Mrs. Adams shifted her weight. She heated flatirons on a wood stove. The wind howled through the broken windows, swept on into the bedroom. A poor idiot child grabbed at Mrs. Adams's skirt and stared up at her. A lean, pocked cat, a joke, a specter of a cat, wound in and out of the table legs. I watched Mrs. Adams's practiced, worn hands unfold the sprinkled clothes, smooth them, and spread them on the table. Her hair tumbled damply around her face. I wondered what she would answer if I said: "Do you know, Mrs. Adams, American women are the most pampered in the world?"

She turned an iron up and went to the stove to stuff cardboard into the firebox. "Coal's gone," she said. "Can't buy no more till we get a check from you all next week."

We talked as she ironed. After a while she said: "Now, have you finished?"

I nodded.

"I ast you because they's a few questions I want to ast you and I didn't want to butt in till you was through. Do you know what it's like to have to tell childern they's nothin' to eat? I got seven childern. All nice childern except this little one here. They'd make out fine if they had enough to eat and enough to wear. Ain't no way in the world to make the re- lief check last till another one's due. I've just give out of ways of tellin' them ain't nothin' to eat and tryin' to git them off to bed without no supper. I thought maybe you could tell me somethin' to tell them."

She looked at me not in anger, not to accuse me, but in the hope of help. I was full of shame.

I felt like a traitor as I closed the door on her and went down the steps.

The wind charged in one great gust and tore my umbrella inside out. The cover sailed like a small black angry cloud down the street. I threw the useless frame into the gutter and ran into the next house.

Mrs. Jackson waved me in. "Didn't start a fire," she explained, "because it's nearly time for me to take my turn watchin' old man Allen. He's mighty sick but he won't let them send him to Grady so the neighbors is takin' turns settin' with him. If you can just get on with what you need to know about me and my circumstances I'll be much obliged to you."

The rain swept down in heavy blows on the house; it spilled through the roof in streams. Mrs. Jackson rushed about setting down buckets and pans to catch the downfall. Above the plopping noise of the rain falling around us we talked.

She glanced at the clock on its side, pointing to eleven thirty, then made a quick calculation and decided it was two forty-five. "If I turnt it back," she said, "like as not it'd stop on me. Clocks is like folks, if you want to get anythin' out of them you might as well do it their way." She tied her head up in a shawl, put on an old felt hat, then over that contrived some kind of covering from a paper sack. "I've got to be leaving," she said. "Now, Miss Wallace, it was plum foolish of you to come out a day like today without no umbreller."

I told her what had happened. "Maybe it was a trial sent to you by the devil," she said. "Well, you certainly can't go out in no such rain as this. You'll be drownded like a rat if you even so much as try to get to the corner to catch a streetcar. You're as welcome as the flowers in May to set here, not much shelter with all these here leaks but I sure want you to feel at home if you've got a mind to stay. I'm ashamed to leave you but I got to go."

She opened a closet and pointed to some magazines. "Maybe they'll hep you pass away the time. Miz Green next door says such trash as I do read and I say to her well, the Lord tells us to seek the truth and it will make us free and every single, solitary word in them books is the truth, sworn to, it says so, and as for myself seein' as how old I am it's right good to read about all the things that coulda happened to me and didn't and it's comfortin' to read about folks that is in a worse shape than I am. Miz Green says as for herself she'd as soon be caught workin' in a whorehouse as to read about such goin's on."

As her farewell gesture she dodged in and out of the streams of rain, grabbed an armful of confession magazines, and dumped them in my lap.

The rain came down harder. The pans and buckets were awash, the room was filled with the dissonance of rain hitting aluminum, tin, iron, wood. I took the pans one by one to the kitchen sink to empty them. I ferreted out a dry place to sit but the rain found my coat collar and dripped down it. I moved, so that I sat halfway in the closet. I began to read, wondering if Gwen had written any of these stories. She had mentioned abortions, illegitimate births, illicit love. I found none of that. Instead in story after story I came upon a kind of emotional striptease.

When Geoff kissed me good-bye, wearing his new uniform and I kissed him in return, a kiss

*that had my soul in it, a kiss that meant he had
my love forever, I did not know he was leaving
behind him misery and dishonor.*

*I remember so well the evening I sat before
my fire, my soft blond curls brushed, my full
lips aching for his, when a knock sounded at
my door.*

A brittle, sophisticated woman stood there.

"I am Geoff's wife," she said.

I read the formula with variations, fascinated;
whatever the girls who wrote the stories were paid,
they earned it. I thought of Gwen, who would soon,
within a few hours, sit down to write one of these
stories, as she had been doing every night for seven
years.

In a little while darkness kept me from reading. I
glanced at the clock and, calculating as Mrs. Jackson
had done, I decided it must be four thirty. While I
was in the neighborhood I wanted to see Mr. Lawrence. I emptied the pots and pans again and returned
them to their strategic places, then I stacked the
confession magazines back in the closet and left.

⊂⊐   ⊂⊐   ⊂⊐

WALKING in the rain I smiled, thinking of
Mr. Lawrence. A few more rain-splashed blocks and
I would be with him in his small house in the slums;
the house where his friends without number found

laughter and tranquillity: an unsure adolescent from across the street, needing help with lessons and parents and girl friends; a crony from Buckhead to re-create the Battle of Peachtree Creek, to bemoan the replacement of Johnston by Hood; the children of his friends; the grandchildren of his friends, all eager to warm themselves in the sun of his kindness and compassion and delicate wit. His little house was bombarded by his friends; still it waited with an eager hospitality for everyone; it appeared never to be full or crowded, but receptive and ready for the next visitor.

Chance and misfortune had taken everything from Mr. Lawrence—his adored wife, his only child, a son, his property, his money, except for the meagerest income. Still he had everything; at seventy-eight his heart was alert to whatever happened, whether on his street or on a continent half a hemisphere away. At seventy he had come to the house in the slums—the only place he could afford—with Andrew, his devoted friend. Together they had made a garden, together they planted roses and shrubbery; then year after year, as arthritis crippled him, Mr. Lawrence had to do his part of the garden work through the open windows of his bedroom. Now all he knew of the garden was what he saw from his bed, the roses that sometimes climbed inside his room from the arbors near his window, the chrysanthemums that Andrew brought in, the sketches Andrew made of the plants and how they bloomed. Twice a year, in spring and in autumn, he made the painful round in Andrew's arms of the lawn and garden. He had been my grandfather's friend; he became my dearest friend and he shared my rabid, unquenchable appetite for detective stories.

Even in going up the steps of the tiny white house a sense of peace and acceptance warmed me. I knocked at the door; a moment later Andrew let me in. I looked with pleasure at his handsome brown face, his tall, erect body, his large, strong hands that showed the hard work he had done all his life, with love and pride and devotion. We smiled and greeted each other.

"Mr. Lawrence will be so happy to see you."

"I'm the happy one."

I went into Mr. Lawrence's room. From his bed he said hello in the most musical voice in the world— Southern, yet without a whine and paying respect to r's and g's. I glanced at his beautiful face and wondered if anywhere else there could be two such handsome faces as his and Andrew's. His eyes twinkled as if my presence were a welcome gift bestowed by the friendliest, most propitious gods.

There was a knock at the front door. We heard Andrew open it; we didn't pretend to talk, each of us was curious about the knock. Soon Andrew came back with a bundle. Mr. Lawrence poked at it, shook it. Outside on the street a motor started; we watched a green truck from Rich's pass.

"I know what the package is," he said. "A delivery truck from Rich's stops, Andrew signs for a package. That means only one thing. I'm so pleased."

Andrew tore the bundle open and books fell out.

"I ordered them for you Friday. They've just been published. I hope they're good." I said.

Andrew held them up. Mr. Lawrence read their titles; his mouth watered as a gourmand's does when he reads a special menu. "*The Daffodil Affair, The Case of the Careless Kitten, Sporting Blood, The Moving Finger.* How nice. I'd exhausted my supply of detective novels and had to resort to this."

His knobby fingers held up *The Odyssey*. He gestured toward a chair. "Do sit by the fire and warm yourself."

I did as he said. "I love this room," I said. "Its beauty, its simplicity." I looked at the bare walls in the palest of yellow, the windows uncurtained so Mr. Lawrence might see out, the chrysanthemums bright yellow and white on the chest of drawers and on a table at my elbow, the two graceful Hitchcock chairs, the comfortable red armchair in which I sat.

"You adorn it," he said.

I glanced at my muddy shoes, my finger peeped through a hole in my glove, my hair was stringy, I hadn't put on lipstick since early morning. I was grateful for his gallantry and told him so.

He looked at the book he held. "Speaking of *The Odyssey*," he said, "do you know that for years I've thought that being between Scylla and Charybdis was being confronted by a dilemma, by equal dangers. Not at all. To be caught in Charybdis's whirlpool was fatal but to pass by Scylla, if you did it at the right time, as Odysseus did, was to suffer loss but not disaster."

He leaned the book on his stomach and flurried

through some pages; he read the passage he had mentioned. "You see, Odysseus and his crew went past Scylla, who snatched some of the men but not all. The ship could continue on its course. It shows you how the edge can be worn from meanings."

In the warmth of his presence I often remembered things I had forgotten; now some of *The Odyssey*, buried long ago in my high school days, came back. "What I disliked about Odysseus," I said, "was the way he treated Penelope when he came home. He revealed himself to his son and his swineherd and his nurse, but Penelope had to wait and she'd been so faithful all those long years."

We said nothing for a time. Coals settled in the fireplace. There came the soothing sound of Andrew's footsteps, the door opened, a teapot's long spout appeared first and Andrew came in with a tray.

Mr. Lawrence thanked Andrew and then he commented on what I had said about Odysseus. "My dear, I suppose in all ages women have waited too long for men to return from wars."

Andrew handed me a cup of tea; I drank from it hungrily, grateful over the way it wandered and spread its heat down my throat.

"Have you had a trying day?" Mr. Lawrence asked.

"No more than usual. I hate to see hunger."

"The stupid thing is that there is enough food for everyone." Then as if to comfort me he said: "You do all that you can."

I finished the tea and handed my cup to Andrew to fill again.

"It's shocking that we seem to be able to do so little," I said.

After a while Andrew took the tray and cups and left us alone.

All that had gone before had been a prelude: the lovers' preliminaries before the real lovemaking begins; Mr. Lawrence and I were ready to settle down to essentials.

"I reread *The Hands of Mr. Ottermole* last night," I said. "Surely it's the best short story of all about murder."

"But no," he said and laughed and his laughter warmed me as much as the hot tea had. "I can't agree. Not when there's such a story as *The Two Bottles of Relish*."

I shuddered, remembering Lord Dunsany's superb story, its deftness, its quiet yet thunderous ending. But I wouldn't agree. "No. *The Hands of Mr. Ottermole* is the best of all. The London atmosphere, the darkness, the suspense, the beauty of the writing. The ending—no one learns but the reader who the murderer is."

Mr. Lawrence smiled; he was not to be shaken. "No. I insist upon *The Two Bottles of Relish*."

We sat grinning at each other, each adamant, each smug in his choice.

"Think of Poe," Mr. Lawrence said. "Think what we owe to him. Think of it. He invented the detective story. Mind you, he invented it."

We thought reverently of Poe and of *Murders in*

the Rue Morgue, The Purloined Letter, The Mystery of Marie Roget.

Then our talk leaped to another facet of detective stories.

"What's your favorite opening?" Mr. Lawrence asked.

I had told him many times. We played this like a game, waiting to catch each other if an opinion had been altered.

"*The Woman in White,* of course. 'This is the story of what a Woman's patience can endure and what a Man's resolution can achieve.' Who would dare skip a word after such an opening?"

"Mine is *Before the Fact,*" Mr. Lawrence said. " 'Some women give birth to murderers, some go to bed with them, and some marry them. Lina Aysgarth had lived with her husband for nearly eight years before she realized that she was married to a murderer.' Now, really, that can't be matched and you know it."

He seemed to waver; he shook his head. "It's true that my favorite opening is *Before the Fact,* but we mustn't forget *Trent's Last Case.* 'Between what matters and what seems to matter, how should the world we know judge wisely?' "

We savored our cherished openings like the bouquet of a fine wine and then we reviewed our recipe for the perfect murder story.

"I think it would have to be set in England," Mr. Lawrence said.

"No trick weapon. Not too much to do with alibis. No love story," I added.

"But we're stupid," Mr. Lawrence said. "The best of every art—and detective fiction is certainly an art —contradicts any rule or pattern anyone might want to impose on it."

"Why do some people detest murder stories?" I asked.

"My dear, I don't know, but it seems to me that between no widely divergent groups—Socialists and Fascists, liberals and conservatives, moderns and classicists—does the gulf yawn as wide as the one dividing those who do read and those who don't read mystery novels."

"Why do people like detective fiction?"

Without hesitating Mr. Lawrence said: "Because it has form, it's intricate, complex—it whets one's interest. We like to read something where everything has meaning."

"But everything doesn't have meaning in mysteries. Many things seem important that aren't."

"At any rate in the end certain points add up. A summing up can be made. Evil recognized. Truth revealed," Mr. Lawrence said.

I saw a chance to repeat my heresy; a week didn't pass that I didn't proclaim it. "I hate Sherlock Holmes," I said. "I'm sorry. I know he's your favorite. But I can't bear him. He's so superior, so bored. And he hounds poor Dr. Watson, makes him seem such a fool."

Mr. Lawrence smiled. "There's no converting you.

Just be sure a Baker Street Irregular doesn't overhear you. Holmes of course is the greatest detective. One of his speeches to Watson is the very essence of everything that is exciting about detective fiction—its expectancy, apprehension. 'Now is the dramatic moment of fate, Watson, when you hear a step upon the stair which is walking into your life, and you know not whether for good or ill.' "

I refused to be won over; I changed the subject. "What happened on August 4, 1892?"

"Lizzie Borden took an axe and gave her mother forty whacks."

"What ends with 'And Winnie inherited twelve hundred a year'?"

"*Payment Deferred.* I read that again last week. How does Forester do it? That miserable little wretch of a man Marble with his adultery, his murder, his obsession about his house, his mistreatment of his wife and children. You hate him and yet you don't want him found out."

"Will there ever be anything as exciting as reading *The Murder of Roger Ackroyd* for the first time?"

"Of course not."

It was time for Mr. Lawrence to question me. "Let's say you can have only one detective story. You have to make a choice. Just one out of all we've read. What would yours be?"

The answer tumbled from my lips. "*The Nine Tailors.* Nothing touches it. What's yours?"

"Do I have to make a choice? There're so many fine ones."

"But you have to make a choice. Come on. I've told you mine."

"Very well. *The Moonstone*. And Miss Drucilla Clack is the most delightful narrator in the whole field of detective fiction."

Our talk was then studded with titles and writers, a long recitative. I looked at my watch; I hated to go but I must. Reluctantly I gathered up my notebook and my bag. I stretched my hands out to the fire one last time.

"What do you really think of murder—death by violence?" I asked.

"I hate it, but I'm afraid that like everybody else if I had a motive I'd be capable of killing."

"Do you really mean that?"

"Yes. I think we're all capable of every sin and passion and crime. And every virtue too."

He told me good-bye and said: "This place won't be so pleasant until you come again." He picked up *Sporting Blood* from the books on his bed.

Andrew came in and moved the lamp closer to Mr. Lawrence. He cleaned Mr. Lawrence's glasses and set them on his nose.

I looked at the two friends, the one tender in his ministrations, the other gently accepting them, each loving the other, each needing the other.

I said good night.

As I left Mr. Lawrence's I noticed the rain had slackened and the wind was less fierce. Town was only a pleasant walk away. I sauntered up Pryor Street toward Peachtree for supper.

At the restaurant the hostess seated me at a tiny table with another woman. The sight of her features, almost identical with Mrs. Patch's, dissolved the warmth and kindliness I felt after my visit to Mr. Lawrence. I must have reminded her of her favorite hag too; she and I developed an immediate enmity, deadly and full of cunning.

"But that's my bread," she hissed at me and pulled a bread plate toward her.

We would glance up belligerently at each other. I could no more keep from looking at her than I could keep from reading anyone's paper next to me on a streetcar. I tried to look at others in the restaurant. The place was filled with women who had come in alone and had been forced to share tables; some attempted conversations, others walled themselves against encroachment by newspapers or magazines or books making parapets around their faces. Here and there shoes were off, lying flat as if they too were exhausted and had to relax, tired beyond endurance. Doors opened, admitting more women to be corralled behind ropes until places were ready. Doors opened emptying women full of meat and two vegetables and choice of salad into the rainy night.

"Will you please pass the salt," I said to the woman

opposite me, which she translated correctly as will you please go to the devil.

"Certainly," she answered. I decoded this as the same to you, my dear chippie.

I looked again at the women around me, some of them poked belligerently at their food, others dipped into it suspiciously, many ate it with sensuous pleasure. I glanced once more at the women waiting behind the ropes, unknown to each other, yet standing closer than lovers embracing.

Hatchet Face's knees kept jabbing me, her feet stomped mine into the floor. After a few minutes I looked at my empty plate with thanksgiving. I wished my companion well, but I hoped that never again in whatever time was allotted to me would I catch a glimpse of her.

Outside at Davison's the Whitehall-Beecher car rushed past me. I decided not to wait for another. I walked down Peachtree to Houston, then to Auburn, to Five Points, Alabama, Hunter. A few doors past Mitchell Street I walked around to the back of our building.

I stood for a while looking up at the third floor. The light in Mrs. Patch's office was out; I was glad that she had gone. A violent rain started falling, splashing me. I ran for the back entrance and walked up the back steps timidly. I found my way down the first floor hall from street lights shining through the windows. I went past the waiting-room, now empty of hungry faces and hungry bodies, to be so full the next day of people asking for food and clothing, hoping

most of all for someone who would really listen to
what they had to say.

On the third floor neon signs from Whitehall Street
threw a few shafts of red light into the office. I found
my stall in what seemed an unexpected place; I had
no sense of distance in the dark. I swung around for
strings to the overhead lights; they weren't where I
had imagined them to be. At last the strings were in
my hands. I turned on two overhead lights and the
tiny desk lamp in my stall.

The rain knocked fiercely at the windows. Against
the attack the windows made rattling, chattering
sounds.

I started to work at once. I dragged out the Budget
Manual and entered new figures on the budget sheets.
These were tasks, I told myself. I would not let my
mind dwell on the figures I entered; I would not let it
balk over the pretense that a human being could exist
on what we allowed in the budgets. Food for one
month was seven dollars and ninety-eight cents. I
eased my conscience with the thought that I hadn't
made the world. I hadn't even made up the Budget
Manual. I was employed to do certain duties. Very
well, I would do those duties. I made out a review
form and wrote the pretentious phrase on it, repeated
by us month after month, year after year: Re-
investigation reveals eligibility requirements 1-A
through 12-A continue as previously reported with
the exception of item 5-A changed as reflected below.
Item 5-A was the budget. Mr. Adams, case 109-
27775-A, would now get eighteen dollars and fifty

cents to see him through one month instead of the eighteen dollars he had been getting. My stomach was full of pot roast. With pot roast sitting pleasantly on one's stomach it was simple to be philosophic about other people's stomachs.

The next case was Mrs. Sara Jones. Well, Mrs. Jones had moved to a cheaper place, hoping that by saving on her rent she would have more for food, but she didn't know that only the reduced amount of rent could be entered on her budget, and so instead of continuing to get sixteen dollars and fifty cents her grant would be reduced to thirteen dollars. Again I reminded myself that I only worked at the Social Service Bureau. I didn't set up its regulations. I had developed a slight discomfort in my stomach. The pot roast at last had the grace to lie uneasily.

The case records mounted. Ten budgets were surely enough for one night, I thought self-righteously; after all they weren't paying me for overtime. I gathered the cases up, each with a review form clipped to it, and walked toward Mrs. Patch's office. Even without her in it I dreaded her office, her lair, the torture chamber where we were all so often flayed by her tongue.

I stood for a long time at her door. Then I entered. The light from the office and the half light from the street didn't reach her desk. I couldn't tell in which basket I should put the cases. I tried to reach her desk lamp; some of the records slid from my hands. I swore gently and pulled at the cord of the overhead light.

There was light then and to spare.

I set the records down in Mrs. Patch's in-basket, wondering whether to shout or whether to run.

Mrs. Patch was in front of me. Her head lay on the desk and her hands were outstretched as if she were taking a brief nap. I watched for her to breathe. Even as I watched I knew she would never breathe again. I looked around. Everything seemed the same as usual. A small pile of records was just out of reach of her hands. She must have been reading them. I noticed that the case record of Charles Williams was on top.

I waited and watched, and then it was as if I became two persons. One wanted to run away, quietly, quickly, to get out of the frightening building, to move away from shadows and death. No one knew I was there. I could sneak out and leave Mrs. Patch to be found by someone else. The other person issued orders. You must call the police. You must wait here for them. You must tell them the little you know. You can't leave her alone.

I turned on all the lights. I made a circuit of all the stalls and turned on the desk lamps. I went to the telephone left connected with the outside after hours. The telephone book jumped from my hands. I scraped it up from the floor and splinters gnawed at my fingers. I tried to find the police-station listing. It was nowhere. I dialed the operator listed as emergency on the first page.

I somehow didn't expect a calm, clear voice to answer; I had thought everyone in the world shared my hysteria.

"I'm sorry," I said. "I'm very sorry but I can't find the number of the police station. I won't be able to talk to them even if you connect me. Will you please call them and tell them to come to the Social Service Bureau? The third floor. They can come up the back stairs."

The calm, clear voice asked a logical question.

"And why should I tell them to go there?"

I said: "Because Mrs. Patch—because someone is dead. Murdered."

I didn't understand why I had said the last word, but somehow I knew it was right. I sat at the telephone thinking of Mrs. Patch sprawled at her desk, dead. My thoughts latched on to that and would not move backward or forward. I heard a sound then, the tiny sound of small rushing feet.

A huge wharf rat ran past me into Mrs. Patch's office.

"You mustn't go in there. You mustn't," I yelled.

He paid no attention. I could hear him scampering around as if he were on a pleasure tour of her office.

I remembered Miss Fitzpatrick then. I told myself I must telephone her.

The bell rang and rang. At last there was an answer.

"Jennifer, do forgive me," the voice begged. "Please forgive me. Do, please." Miss Fitzpatrick talked compulsively. "I've been waiting so long for you to call— right here by the telephone so I could answer you immediately. I've sat for hours and hours. I'll come for you right away. I had to get a glass of water—I'm so sorry you had to wait for me to answer—so sorry—

more than I can tell you. I wouldn't have had it happen. It won't happen again. I'll be there in a few minutes—I—"

I had to stop her.

"Miss Fitzpatrick, listen. This is Jane Wallace, one of the workers at the Bureau. I want you to be calm. Please sit down. There's been an accident. Your sister-in-law has been hurt badly. I'm afraid she's dead. You're not to worry. Everything will be all right. The police know about it. They'll be here soon. There's no need for you to come."

The strangest sounds I had ever heard came to me. I couldn't tell whether they were hysterical weeping or hysterical laughter.

⊏⊨ ⊏⊨ ⊏⊨

I WENT to the window farthest from Mrs. Patch's office and Mrs. Patch's dead body to wait for the police. Below a streetcar passed half filled, its passengers hunched over from tiredness, some with bundles stacked high on their laps, some with newspapers spread in cramped fashion before their staring eyes. Tomorrow the papers would have news of the murder. Perhaps the little man I looked at, who glanced at the window where I stood, would say, I passed by there on my way home from work soon after the murder, even before the police had come. The traffic light changed and changed again, still the streetcar

did not move, and the passengers made craning movements to find out why they were stalled. A policeman
appeared. With the authority of his whistle and large
white gloved hands he goaded the traffic into con-
vulsive jerks.

The rain muffled the street sounds, silencing the
comforting noises that would have made the dead not
seem so deathly. The police didn't come, they might
never come. I would wait out the long night with Mrs.
Patch stretched out on her desk, lying in that semblance of sleep. The wharf rat still scampered about,
bolder and bolder, rushing in and out of the stalls,
bounding into Mrs. Patch's office, owning the place.

I waited. I listened. I made threats and devised
strange, wild plans. If the police hadn't come by the
time the traffic light changed seven times I would go
down to the street and wait. I counted the light
changes. Another streetcar inched past. I watched automobiles bogged down in traffic, hands mashed idi-
otically on horns, heads shot out of rapidly descending
car windows to shout or swear. A traffic jam was the
proving ground of the human race's insanity.

Then I forgot the street; the police came.

They filled the place although there were only a few
of them. A photographer was along; bulbs kept flash-
ing. He kneeled, then stood on a chair, as if alter-
nately worshipful and disdainful in the presence of
death. Someone sat near me with a notebook and
someone else asked questions. He didn't once indulge
himself in a declarative sentence; everything was a
question. He started by calling me lady, then pro-

gressed to little lady. I told him my name was Jane
Wallace.

"Yes, little lady, we've got that," he said.

I wasn't sure of anything, the time I had come to
the office, the time I had worked, the time I had found
Mrs. Patch, the time between finding her and tele-
phoning the operator. The little-lady man wouldn't
condone my lapse in memory.

"Now, little lady, of course you can remember. Just
tell me what you did tonight and when."

I began to calculate frantically. I had left Mr. Lawrence's house about six or six thirty and had walked
to Peachtree and Ellis. That must have taken twenty
minutes. Then another twenty minutes to eat. I had
walked back to the office. I must have got back to the
office some time around seven. I had done ten budgets
and had written out ten review forms, say ten to
twelve minutes each. I told him all that.

"That's fine, little lady. Funny how you can remember things when you really want to remember them,
isn't it, little lady?"

Two men walked past with a litter. I turned to
watch Mrs. Patch leave the agency for the last time.

"I guess that's all for tonight," the man said. "We'll
need you tomorrow at the Court House for an inquiry.
Come about ten." He scribbled something on a card
and handed it to me. "That's the room number. See
you then."

As if we had been guests somewhere or on a date
together he took cordial leave and said good night.
"Oh," he called after me like a mother admonishing a

child to take a handkerchief, "stay where we can get in touch with you. I suppose you're in the phone book."

I nodded, shaken to think I might be suspect, and went out ahead of him. As my heels clanked against the iron steps I heard him giving someone instructions to stay there until morning.

Mrs. Patch's descent had been slow. I got to the street just as her bearers reached the ambulance. The wind lifted the sheet covering her; I looked again upon her gross features. Death had brought no peace to them; like a bitter caricaturist death had exaggerated their brutality, emphasized their cruelty.

The familiarity of the world stunned me. It seemed strange that the traffic lights still turned red, amber, and green, that people passed in the same swift way, that paperboys shouted headlines in the same ominous, unintelligible manner, crooking papers so that in passing one could not possibly check up on what they shouted about.

I wanted to talk to someone. I needed most desperately to talk to someone. I thought of Peg. A streetcar came; I clambered on; I swung on an iron pole directly behind the motorman's seat while I shoved around in the labyrinth of my bag for fare. I asked for a transfer; at the Candler Building I got off and walked over to Forsyth across from the Library to wait for the Druid Hills car. One came at last.

A woman on the seat ahead of me yapped. "I will say I have been an exceptional daughter-in-law, my mother-in-law told me so again and again. Well, I could only wish that my own daughter-in-law showed me a little consideration. Do you think she'll let me and David be alone together for a single minute? Let him come over to the house to see me, let him go to my kitchen for a drink of water and do you think she will let me exchange one word with my own son alone? Let him say, Mama, let's go for a ride and she gets in the front seat and I have to shout at him from the back seat whatever I want to tell him. I would like to see him alone just once. I would like to say one word to him that his wife knows nothing about. I can't call him at his office it's against the rules and just let me call him at home and I know his wife is breathing down his neck listening to every word I say. She acts as if she owns him. Nothing like that happens when I call Betty, you can just bet. Why, Betty will tell her husband to go to hell she wants to talk to me privately. She says, Mama, you are my mother and there is no stronger tie than that. Never a word was spoken as true as the old saying, a daughter's a daughter all the days of her life, a son's a son till he gets him a wife. Why last Sunday afternoon—"

A couple got on with a tired little boy, about two. His parents suffered under the dread necessity of showing him off.

"What says moo?" the man asked and made a moo sound.

The child's head bounced back, trying to shake off sleep. "Cow," he said and closed his eyes.

"What says meow?" the woman asked, plowing her head into the child's neck. "What says meow?"

From the outskirts of sleep the dutiful child said: "Kitty."

Across from me a man groaned. "My God," he said. "My God. Women. Mothers-in-law. Parents. The world is being blown to hell, thousands are cremated every day, yet old biddies like that still carry on at the same old stand." He pointed at the mother-in-law. "And look at that poor child. He needs sleep. Yet he's made to perform like an animal act. With parents like that he'll either be the greatest psychotic of all time or he'll build up so much resistance he'll turn out to have as much feeling as a dish of cold grits."

I felt sick. The pot roast was giving me trouble again. I opened a window. "Please"—a wrinkled mummy of a woman leaned over from somewhere in the back and started coughing—"I can't stand any winter wind. My doctor forbids it."

I pulled the window down, the heat and voices from the car choked me. I wondered if Mrs. Post had written a chapter or even a paragraph anywhere on how to be sick on a streetcar. Did one try to vomit quietly in one's pocketbook? Need put me beyond etiquette; I rang the bell to get off. Just in time I found a nice quiet gutter down which the rain sent a small, vigorous whirlpool.

When the pot roast and I had parted without too much regret I noticed I had got off much farther out Ponce de Leon than I had thought. Peg's house would be only a short walk in the dark, heavy rain.

And then I noticed that a car followed me, almost

timidly, like a mongrel who trots far behind and stops when someone turns to watch him, and fear spread with the rain down my body, drowning me, possessing me.

◧ ◧ ◧

THE rain seeped through my coat, somehow it found its devious way inside my galoshes. I turned off the street and walked around to the back of a huge house to a small one that had once been lived in by servants and was now rented by Peg. I knocked at the door, longing for the moment when I might enter.

Through the window I watched Joe and Bill, the two black French poodles, wearing small straw hats and jogging about the living-room on their hind legs. At my knock they turned and walked like sedate, slightly tipsy butlers to the back of the house. Peg came to the door and let me in. Joe and Bill had again changed character; this time they were nosy spinsters waiting to know what the stranger at the door had in mind; then all three, the dogs and Peg, looked at me and sensed I was disturbed. Joe and Bill became what they were—intelligent sympathetic animals; Peg helped me to a chair. The dogs plopped down at a respectful distance from my feet while Peg sat in a chair near me.

I looked at the room. The tender, suffering, wise

faces of the Rouault portraits, The Three Judges, The Old King, The Circus Dancer, were reflected in the three living faces around me. Another wall held four large charcoal sketches Bea had done of clients and had given to Peg; these too were at peace with the Rouault oils and with Peg and the dogs. The rooms were somehow like Mr. Lawrence's, bare, gracious, restful, the rooms of a person who has dispensed with clutter and non-essentials. Peg bent to light the fire. Joe and Bill watched attentively; they seemed to approve of her graceful, effortless movements. Soon I was alone in the room. There was no sensation of being left. Peg and the dogs went quietly, Peg carrying my coat, each dog with a galosh in his mouth. Before I knew it Peg entered with a tray and set it on my knees.

"You look sick, as if you have an upset stomach. There's nothing like tea for it."

Peg was quite right; the tea soothed the empty, querulous places where the pot roast had been. I wanted to talk, to tell everything that had happened.

"I found her dead at her desk," I said, "Mrs. Patch." I told Peg all I remembered, chattering foolishly about the woman at the restaurant, the rat in Mrs. Patch's office, the man who called me little lady, the conversations I overheard on the streetcar.

After a long time Peg said: "I can't be sorry. Every day Mrs. Patch killed self-respect, spirits, souls—whatever it is that's the best part of a person."

The dogs escorted her to the wood basket, supervised while she threw two sticks on the fire. "How awful it must have been for you—finding her," she said.

Peg knew what to do. She moved quietly to the telephone, pulled it with her into her bedroom, shut the door; only now and then a word crept through. She was calling people at the agency, beginning with Mrs. Martin. I had finished the tea when she came back.

"Let's go to see Miss Fitzpatrick," I said. "She may need someone."

"Yes, we must. Then you come back here and spend the night."

"I want to go home."

"Then I'll see that you get to bed. Do you have anything in that Victorian set-up beside sherry?" She knew I didn't; even as she spoke she tucked a bottle into her coat pocket.

Joe and Bill hopped into the back seat and settled themselves at once. We rode for a short while when Peg asked: "What was it like—finding Mrs. Patch?"

"I don't want to think about it."

She insisted. "What was it like? You've got to think about it."

"I want people alive. I don't like to see them dead."

"You say that, knowing the way she treated everyone?"

"There must have been reasons for the way she acted."

"My sympathy goes to her victims."

"She's a victim now."

Our talk reached an impasse. We said no more as

we drove by large houses, their façades like masks hiding whatever there was of joy or unhappiness inside.

At last Peg said: "This must be it." We were on Peachtree in front of a house that sat back huge and dark from the street.

Bill and Joe didn't protest when we left them in the car and walked up the slippery brick walk to the house.

We rang the bell and waited. There was no answer. Peg shoved the door open and called to Miss Fitzpatrick.

"Just a minute. Just a minute, please—as soon as I can find my robe I'll be downstairs."

A light flashed on overhead, a great globe of a light dangling high up on the ceiling, making us blink. Miss Fitzpatrick leaned in pathetic dependence on the banister and made a slow descent as if she stood on a treacherous incline.

"I haven't known what to do—whether to wait up or go to bed. I suppose the police will come." She had reached the hall and grabbed at Peg. "You were so kind to me last night—so very kind. I don't know how to thank you. Oh, my, this time last night we were all so happy and now this awful thing has happened."

Peg looked at me and said: "Jane is the one who found Mrs. Patch and telephoned you."

Miss Fitzpatrick stared at me and then led us from the hall into a large room overloaded with heavy furniture. Pieces of bric-a-brac seemed to shove and crowd each other for space on every possible surface;

the floor was dotted with innumerable small rugs; the walls had an epidemic of framed photographs and pictures hanging drunkenly, unevenly, as if longing to pitch themselves on the floor; the windows wore shrouds of deep-green draperies.

Miss Fitzpatrick selected the most uncomfortable chair in the room, a straight-backed, horsehair monstrosity, and began to talk without looking at us. Her hands wrapped and unwrapped around each other; her head nodded as if to reassure herself; her voice had a deadly sound, almost without stress or accent; the words she spoke were the compulsive doggerel of an idiot.

"She's dead. She's dead. She's dead. Do wishes kill people? There wasn't a moment I didn't wish her dead, dying slowly, in agony, wishing I had the courage to kill her. And now that it's happened I've been weeping for her, forgetting the misery, forgetting what she did to my brother, forgetting what she did to me. I've been weeping for her. Ever since Miss Wallace telephoned I've been crying. How dare I forget? How dare I weep one tear for her?"

The old clock had dominated the room with its rasping ticking; now it took full possession, tearing the room with ten strokes.

The strokes ended.

Miss Fitzpatrick smiled; her mind seemed to dismiss the murder. Joy sat timidly on her features, ready to scamper. "You know, I've been thinking what I could do. I don't imagine Jennifer left me any money, though it may come to me. It should. It be-

longed to my brother. Maybe I could rent out part of
this house. I've longed to do that. Time and again
they've come, young couples wanting rooms, just married, about to be separated by the war. Here it was,
this whole big house empty except for the two of us
but she wouldn't hear of having anyone come. Now
perhaps I can help. Jennifer didn't want love or
kindness or affection."

Weeping racked her again; the pleasure of planning
left her. Peg and I sat there aimlessly.

Peg said: "I know some people who want rooms.
I'll send them around. And we'll tell others at the
agency."

Silence lay heavily around us; I tried futilely to
think of something to say. Peg asked Miss Fitzpatrick
if she wouldn't go home with her for the night.

"No thank you," she answered. "That's most kind
but I must stay here. I really must."

Miss Fitzpatrick walked to the front door with us.
We said good night. Miss Fitzpatrick said again: "I
can't thank you for your kindness. You've been so
thoughtful. So very, very kind."

The rain came down hard, marooning us from Peg's
car, making the distance to it forbidding.

"Let's wait a minute," Peg said.

We walked to the end of the porch and stuck out
our hands to gauge the rain. A light clicked on in the
room where we had sat. We turned toward the light
and could not keep from looking through the window.

Miss Fitzpatrick had entered. Like a dervish she
started moving, shoving pictures from the mantel and

walls, sweeping clutter from the tables; all these small crashes united into deafening sounds. She began to do a little dance, around, through, and over the debris; her hair fell from its tight knot; a smile sat weirdly on her tear-stained face. And then through the door a large black cat leaped and sat on the back of a chair. He started spitting at Miss Fitzpatrick, pawing the silk back of the chair. Miss Fitzpatrick crouched against the wall; two pictures jumped from the wall and fell at her feet. Her hands flew up as guards and she whimpered.

Peg left me. I saw her enter the room and grab the cat. Soon Peg was back on the porch; in the darkness I saw her toss a darker mass, there was a thud, then sounds of movement on the soggy leaves, and the cat raced up a tree.

"Did you see how that cat intimidated Miss Fitzpatrick?" Peg asked. "I was about ready to believe in the transmigration of souls. I thought Mrs. Patch had come back in the form of her cat."

She dashed out in the rain to her car and ran back, followed by Joe and Bill. I stayed on the porch and watched through the window as Peg led the dogs toward Miss Fitzpatrick; each of the women took a dog and brushed the streaming rain from his coat. Peg stood quietly over the dogs then and pointed toward Miss Fitzpatrick. Joe and Bill understood they were to watch over her, to care for her. They assumed their duties with much dignity, walking with confidence toward her; she received them with caressing pats.

In a little while we got in Peg's car; I was too exhausted to care that a car followed us, that it stopped four doors from the house where I lived.

Peg helped me upstairs and busied herself getting my bed ready while I bathed. I dried myself indifferently, put on my pajamas and climbed on the couch. Peg handed me a glass. "It's nearly neat, so hold on."

I drank while she turned toward the books.

"*The Glass Key, The Murder of My Aunt, Murders in Volume II, The Lodger, The Beast Must Die, The Crime of Laura Sarelle.* Don't you have anything but murder stories? This is one night you aren't going to read one."

"Please shut up," I said. "You talk like a crank about detective stories."

She found something else. Her eyes looked at it with unbelief as she pulled out a collection of poetry. "Where on earth did this come from?"

I tried to be witty or at least apt, and to say I must have borrowed it and had forgotten to return it, but the whisky had paralyzed my tongue. I gulped the last of the whisky; for a second the furniture seemed to leap around me. I grasped the couch while it rode some waves; then everything settled down. I felt benevolent, omniscient, omnipotent, and very, very drowsy.

Peg's voice came to me from far across the room, a continent away.

Come Sleep, O Sleep, the certain knot of peace,
   The baiting place of wits, the balm of woe,
The poor man's wealth, the prisoner's release,
   Th' indifferent judge between the high and low;

With shield of proof, shield me from out the prease
  Of these fierce darts, Despair at me doth throw . . .

There were other words I didn't hear. The soft,
pleading words spoken in Peg's soothing voice lulled
me. I dozed and half waked. I heard the faint whisper
of pages turning, and then her voice again.

O soft embalmer of the still midnight,
  Shutting, with careful fingers and benign,
Our gloom-pleased eyes, embowered from the light,
  Enshaded in forgetfulness divine:
O soothest Sleep! if so it please thee, close
  In midst of this thine hymn my willing eyes . . .

Her voice became a *berceuse*, then music with indis-
tinct words. Soon there was silence. My door clicked
shut and Peg was gone.

I slept.

   ✠ ✠ ✠

   I WAKED and started the serious, automatic business of getting off to work. I had folded the top sheet
and was about to stack it in the closet with the blan-
kets when I remembered Mrs. Patch's death. I sat
down on the couch and crumpled the sheet in my lap,
as if the postponement of the morning's routine might
put off the fact of her murder. I began the familiar
program again. My body followed the patterns, yet it

seemed strange that each task was to be done as usual in spite of Mrs. Patch. The egg yolk stuck no less hard to the plate because she was dead, the milk bottle still had to be washed, the garbage emptied. Details made no concession to her death; they intruded, demanding their usual attention.

Every chore was at last done; no more delay was possible. I picked up the *Constitution*. Mrs. Patch had replaced world events in the headlines. A stranger looked out at me from the front page: myself. I read about myself with a peculiar kind of wonder and disbelief, disclaiming myself, unwilling somehow to acknowledge I was the one who had discovered Mrs. Patch and had talked to the police, was probably being followed by them. After I had read the account of the murder three times I looked again and again at my picture, forgetting the reason it was there, ignoring the death that gave it prominence. I wished that my mouth had shown up better; and my eyebrows, surely they were darker than the faint lines I saw before me.

After a while my ego subsided enough to let me dress and leave the house.

The rain had stopped; in its place came a wind that tore through trees and bones. I shivered waiting for a streetcar. One came and passed on, loaded, with no room for more passengers. When the next car came the conductor said good morning to me and mentioned that he hadn't seen me for some time. I couldn't answer that with luck I didn't get his car because it made me late to work. He said he hoped things were fine with me and I thanked him and said yes and the same to him, wondering as I spoke how the tongue can remember the appropriate clichés in times of stress.

I walked up the aisle, choked with people, and as I tried to get a handhold and toehold I looked with envy at those sitting down. Papers were spread out. As I glanced at my picture staring from the papers I felt undressed, naked among all those people with coats buttoned high. No one noticed me. No one connected my face with the one on the front page. No one paid the slightest attention; they all read with no more than the usual early-morning interest and turned quickly to the comics.

Their indifference coddled me until I got to the agency. The street outside was jammed with clients; the waiting-room was packed. The excitement was epidemic; voices leaped into hysteria. Conversation was studded with mention of that old woman, that old Mrs. Patch, that boss lady. Somebody moaned. Somebody shouted: "I reckon they'll close down this place. I reckon they'll take everything away from us and shut it down for good."

I tried to get in the front entrance; I was dashed back and forth by a wave of humanity and at last swept back to the street. I went around to the back of the building. The crowd was there too. A finger pointed at me, waggled underneath my nose.

"That's the one that found her," a man said. "Do you reckon she done it? I wouldn't put a thing past a one of them up here the way they're always actin' like God amighty. What I say is what goes over the devil's

back is sure to come under his belly. Would serve
'em right if they hung the whole bunch of 'em up
here."

I got past the nightmare of faces. The workers were
all upstairs talking; I heard their voices from the hall.
I entered and they stopped as if their conversation
was beyond my understanding. They said hello much
too politely; it recalled to me the way we had spoken
to Mary when she came back to the office on Monday, the first time she had come since word had been
received that her husband had been killed. I might
have had a disease that it wasn't polite to mention in
public, the way they were determined not to talk
about Mrs. Patch to me; everyone said something
strained about the weather.

In a little while Mrs. Martin called me to her office.
I told her all that I had to tell. She thanked me for
what I had done and how I had acted. Later there
was a brief staff meeting of everyone in the agency.
Mrs. Martin said we were to answer all questions the
police asked and help them in every possible way;
aside from that we were to go about our work as usual.
We still had the deadline to meet on Friday. We were
to talk quite openly with the clients; they were naturally interested in Mrs. Patch's death.

At ten I went to the Court House. The man who
called me lady and little lady was there. As on the
night before he called me lady at first, then settled on
little lady.

There was a great deal of talk from a number of
persons. I had my say in a voice that didn't belong to

me; I didn't want to claim my trembling hands or the uneasy way I sat on the chair when I talked.

The conclusion of the hearing was official but not new. Mrs. Patch had met death at the hand of a person unknown. She had died of severe injuries to her skull. A bronze paperweight on her desk had been used as the weapon; there were many smeared fingerprints on it, but the only clear ones were her own.

The man said twice: "You can go now, little lady. Much obliged." We were alone in the large room. I told him good-bye and then had trouble finding the door.

Outside in the hall three men talked earnestly. One replaced large photographs in an envelope. Pictures of Mrs. Patch's dead face went out of sight as I ran toward the elevator.

On Pryor Street I walked two blocks in the direction of the agency. All at once I knew I couldn't return just then. I had to get to Mr. Lawrence.

⚿ ⚿ ⚿

I STOOD in front of Mr. Lawrence's house, feeling that I had come upon a haven; tension and anxiety left me. I knocked lightly on the front door. Andrew might have been waiting for me; his answer was immediate.

He smiled his friendly smile and said: "Mr. Lawrence and I are afraid you've been having a bad time."

"Thank you for thinking about me," I said.

Andrew placed a chair for me close to Mr. Lawrence's bed. He greeted me from a mass of pillows and said: "Let's talk about it."

I told him what had happened since I had left his quiet house the night before.

"Most of what you've said has been in the papers and on the radio. What I want is for you really to tell me about it—the people at your agency—what's been going on there. Everything."

Mrs. Patch's pettiness and cruelty spilled out of my mouth; I related incident after incident.

"And her behavior had been going on a long time?"

"As long as she's been at the agency."

"Nothing is more shocking than bad manners," he said. "Did her behavior get worse in these last few days?"

"I don't think so."

"But something must have happened. After all, she hadn't been murdered before. I'm assuming that someone at your agency murdered her."

Mr. Lawrence's words stunned me. I hadn't thought of the murderer; the fact of the murder had monopolized my mind. Now I knew that one of us had killed her, one of us in anger, or perhaps not in anger but craftily and with malice. I thought of my friends; one by one they seemed to smile at me: Gwen, Mary, Peg, Margy, Smitty, Bea, Miss Reeves, Mrs. Martin, all smiled at me, knowing I would smile back, exonerating them in my mind.

"Someone in your agency decided—as Thomas

Burke described it—'to usurp the awful authority of nature and destroy a human being.' Who could it have been?"

"It couldn't have been anyone."

He ignored my answer. He wrote down the names of everyone in our district; he made a chart of the office, labeling the stalls with our names.

"Gwendolyn Pierce is the first one on the right as you enter. Let's begin with her," he said.

"Gwen. What can I say about her? She's generous with her money but not so generous with her time. She makes lots of money writing confession stories."

"What do you mean about being generous with her money but not with her time?"

"She's lavish in making contributions to hospital funds, the Community Chest, things like that. But she doesn't offer to do any extra work around the office when anyone is sick. I'm afraid I'm being a cat."

I went on talking self-consciously about them all; Miss Reeve's outburst; Mary's grief; the way wild, unaccountable things happened to Bea; Smitty's interest in psychiatry; Margy's ineffectualness.

"Now tell me more about Mrs. Patch."

"I really don't know what to say about her. I've told you the way she acted. She had a child's capacity for finding the word that hurt, of finding the feature or characteristic you're most ashamed of."

"Tell me about her good points. We're destroyed by our virtues as often as we're destroyed by our vices."

"She didn't have any."

"Come now. That's not true. And I have another

man named Laurence to back me up—however, he
spelled his name with a *u* instead of a *w*. Anyway he
said: 'For nought so vile that on the earth doth live,
But to the earth some special good doth give.' "

"I can't remember a single kind thing she ever did."
I didn't talk for a moment; then I said grudgingly:
"I suppose she was honest about money. I mean honest
in the way she went over the budgets to be sure we
were accurate, to be positive that no client got more
than the absolute minimum."

Mr. Lawrence closed his eyes as if he were ab-
sorbing all I had said. He asked me about the building,
the other workers besides those in our section, their
duties and relationship to Mrs. Patch. He wanted to
know everything that had happened at the agency
during the week. I recalled Monday morning, beginning with Peg and me standing at the window watching everyone come in, watching the rain. I told Mr.
Lawrence everything I could remember, the conversations I had had, the food I'd eaten, the visits I had
made to clients, the way I reacted to everything.

"You seem to have a photographic memory," he said
when I had finished. "Not that exactly, but you remember the way people say things and what they say
and do. You remember atmosphere."

"We all do that in social work," I said. "We have to.
We have to pay attention to what's said and what we
see. It's part of our job."

"Tell me about the kind of person who does social
work."

"As many different kinds are in it as in every other

profession. There's no typical social worker. There're just as many misfits and fools and asses in social work as in anything else. And just as many fine persons."

He grinned at my answer and said: "In which category do you place yourself?"

I grinned back at him. "First one and then another," I said.

"But why was Mrs. Patch murdered?" he asked. "Let's think. We've read enough about murder."

I thought of the detective stories I'd read in the last month.

"She was a threat. The victim is always a threat to the murderer." Then I recalled the introduction to *Murder for Pleasure.* "Roughead says he never saw a murderer who wasn't an egomaniac."

Mr. Lawrence said: "Doesn't it take egomania to live, to push one's pathetic small self about one's business?"

Then he came back to the terrifying question: "Do you really think it was one of you?"

My tongue had difficulty with the answer my brain sent it. I said, stammering: "I don't see how it could be anyone else."

"Let's not say it's impossible that anyone else did it. The effect of such a woman would go everywhere. Not just in your agency but everywhere she went, everything and everyone she touched would be involved in her evil."

"Especially her sister-in-law."

"Yes, especially Miss Fitzpatrick."

I thought of her terrified behavior, the agony of anxiety that was her life.

"No, Miss Fitzpatrick couldn't have done the murder," I said. "It must have been one of us."

"Then someone you like or someone you love did it."

I made no answer.

"Let's go back to last night. What did you feel when you found Mrs. Patch?"

I relived the moments, I was caught up in their dread. I mounted the stairs, I reached for the lights, I figured the budgets. The time came for me to remember picking up case records and taking them to Mrs. Patch's office. I looked down at her outstretched hands, at her head bent in death. All the emotions came back.

"Terror. Panic. I was paralyzed. I wanted to leave, to pretend I hadn't found her."

"Yet you knew you had to do the little that you could."

"Yes, but I put it off as long as I could." I remembered going to the window, looking down on the street at the traffic, watching the lights change, watching people pass.

"What did you think as you waited for the police to come?"

"I remembered how unkind and unpleasant she had been and yet I didn't like to think of her as dead, as being murdered. I thought. 'This is the first time I've seen Mrs. Patch helpless. This is the first time she's been a victim.' "

"At last she knew what it was to be a mouse in eternity."

I didn't understand. I repeated what he said, but as a question: "A mouse in eternity?"

"Yes. That's a line from some verses I think of often.

> *It is very, very curious*
> *How one may either be*
> *A cat that nibbles a moment*
> *Or a mouse in eternity.*

Mrs. Patch was someone who had nibbled for many moments. Last night something happened to make her a mouse in eternity. Why?"

I had no answer.

"Shall we try to find out?"

"Yes," I said.

We smiled at each other but our smiles did not last; they were erased by the awful fact that I must try to track down and betray a friend.

❦ ❦ ❦

MRS. PATCH's office had been unsealed by the police when I got back from talking to Mr. Lawrence. Mrs. Martin entered it as if Mrs. Patch were on vacation and her work must be attended to; she showed no dread, no revulsion. She read cases, approved budgets and review forms, then left to return to her own office, saying we were to let her know when she could be of help to us.

Our watches ticked on toward the time of Mrs. Patch's funeral; so soon dead, so soon to be buried; even the day before she had been among us, her tongue had scourged us in fury, her anger had worn away at our self-respect; now we felt nothing but the dreadful gap of her absence.

At a quarter of three the usual bustle about leave-taking was muffled. We put on hats and coats as if the dead were in our midst; there were whispers about who would ride with whom.

Ted was downstairs waiting for Margy. Bea and Miss Reeves went with them; Gwen and I got a ride with Peg. Mary wasn't in; we imagined she would go directly to the service from her district.

We walked into the chapel full of roars from an organ and almost empty of people. We crept in, on tiptoe, sneaking in on death so we wouldn't arouse his ire. The lilies crowded in on us, they clamped down on our noses like ether cones to anæsthetize us. The minister was there; he was simply there, no one saw him enter, and he began to talk. Again the transition was too much; Mrs. Patch had been alive the day before and now she was dead, murdered, her torrent of abuse was forever stopped.

I tried not to listen to the eulogy, though some of the words leaked through my barricade of inattention. . . . a life dedicated to the service of others . . . a believer in meeting the hungers of mankind . . . devoted to the poor, the sick, the aged.

Peg made a gesture of distaste, then pulled a small envelope from the rack in the bench ahead of us and wrote an obscene word.

Again, I shut out the minister's speech. Again the fact of Mrs. Patch's death clubbed me into disbelief. I thought: "Mrs. Patch is dead; last week, even yesterday, she was among us, capable of many kinds of acts, yet always choosing to do the most hated and hateful." I wondered what had molded her, what cancerous hate she had been near that she absorbed it and multiplied it so that she would die without having a single person to mourn her, no one to weep, no one to say in agony: "What will I do without her?" My thoughts rushed on; her death had made headlines and yet she wasn't dead to all places; her name still appeared in the telephone book, on mailing lists, on our agency letterheads. Tomorrow a letter might come to her asking her to contribute to something, or to buy something at a tremendous saving, or perhaps an acquaintance would write from somewhere far away where her murder hadn't been in the papers: *Dear Jennifer*—did anyone anywhere call her by her first name except her sister-in-law?—*Dear Jennifer, I was happy to have your letter and am sorry not to have written sooner but*—What kind of a child had Mrs. Patch been? It was impossible to imagine her as a child; trusting, anxious, eager for love and approval; she must have sprung full-grown from some school of social work.

The man droned on. In the pulpit her life sounded noble. Even on paper it sounded all right. Her career had been in social work; she had headed a large agency in the West but came south because the South was where she felt the greatest need existed for social services. She had married twice. She had supported her sister-in-law since her first husband's death. She worked hard; overtime every day. She never missed any time from work because of illness. I had heard enough. I wanted the man to shut up. Soon I felt he would say that she ate Swiss cheese sandwiches for lunch with mustard on one side and mayonnaise on the other and that she drank her coffee with cream but no sugar.

I counted noses of the reluctant funeral guests; two or three from the Children's Division; Mrs. Martin sat with Miss Fitzpatrick; some people from four or five of the other social agencies in town; Miss Reeves just ahead, Margy and Ted, Bea, Peg, Gwen, and I.

A thought tore at my brain. Somewhere in the chapel was Mrs. Patch's murderer. And what about that person's thoughts? What must she be thinking as we were all gathered because of her fatal act? Perhaps: "God, why did I come? I had to come. They would have noticed if I hadn't. Last night one moment she was alive. The next moment she was dead and I had killed her. I struck down a human being and because of me they are all here and she lies on the platform and that man is saying flagrant lies about her. If he only knew what she had done, what she was going to do to me, what she had done to me. I hated her. We all hated her. I didn't know this time yesterday that soon I would pick up her cherished paperweight and bludgeon her to death. I hadn't known it takes such small effort to crush a skull. I'm safe. I'll stay safe. No one can know that it was me. They all wanted her dead. They are guilty too. By chance I carried out their wishes."

I wondered what her name was who might be having those thoughts. I wondered what dreams she had dreamed the night before and would dream the rest of her life.

Gwen nudged me. Everyone else had risen. I jumped up and followed the procession outside. Ted and Margy were on the steps of the chapel; everything was still in the slow hush of ceremony. Margy was weeping; Miss Reeves wept, everywhere handkerchiefs jabbed at eyes. For a moment I was convinced that I had been mistaken in thinking Mrs. Patch had no mourners; many were weeping for her, and then I knew they did not weep for her but for death that waits eternally for life and comes with such suddenness. Ted made an inept attempt to comfort Margy by patting her shoulder. No one spoke, as if speaking were indecent so near to death.

Quiet held us; we might have taken the vow of silence. No one spoke on the way back to the agency. In the parking lot we got out of the car and still didn't speak.

As we entered the Bureau and pushed our way in the crowded halls I thought: "Nothing has changed, nothing has really changed."

From the waiting-room came the receptionist's kind voice: "And what do you want to see about, Mr. Brown?"

"I aim to register a complaint. You all give old man Suggs that drinks his relief check up a mattress. I had my order for a mattress in for six months and I ain't seen no sign of a mattress and by God he had a mattress and here he come a-haulin' one in a hand cart yestiddy sayin' you all give it to him and here he is sleepin' on two mattress so hep me God and me sleepin' on a pallet made outta shucks and a rat eat up quilt. I aim to make a full investigation and if I don't git satisfaction right quick I'm goin' right on over to the guvner's office."

A jug of a woman, all body and lip, screamed: "That's the truth, that's the way you all carry on up here, give every form thang to one and don't give nothin' to the rest."

Listening to the clients, we were tossed back from the solemn contemplation of death to the fierce, desperate, wonderful reality of life.

Upstairs we went to our stalls and collected notebooks, then in slow procession we left again to make home visits. As I waited for a streetcar I went down my file of reviews still to be made; it was four o'clock; I was tired. I would make one visit to Mr. Jones, come back to the office and fill out some forms, then go home and rest.

Later I found the gaping door of the drafty barn of a house where Mr. Jones lived.

A woman came out and I asked her if Mr. Jones was in.

She said: "Who wants to know?"

I told her.

"I might uv knowed it," she said. "You all stand out like sore thumbs. Can tell you a mile off. Them felt hats, them gloves, them low-heel shoes, them little black books."

She turned her back on me and bellowed, "Paw, here's yore vizter."

From far down the hall Mr. Jones let out a mournful My God, then he let out an indignant My God. After a while he came to the front door.

"Well, come on in if you've got to," he said.

I followed him to a small back room. He shoved a bottomless chair toward me and ran his thumbs under his suspenders. One great wave of tobacco juice leaped from his mouth into the fire. His right thumb still held on to a suspender but he raised his hand so that he could smooth the drippings from his chin.

"Strikes me as the damndest most tom fool way in the world to make a livin', the way you make yores, goin' out devilin' people with all them questions. Don't get shed of you one time till you're right back on the doorstep. Yall hant people like hants hant a graveyard. Yes, sir, the way you all hound me you would think I was tryin' to make off with all the cash in the United States Treasury."

Another spurt of tobacco almost put out the fire.

"If it ain't against yore reggerlations would you let

me know when you're due back? I want to mark it
down on the calendar. I want to know for shore how
much peace I got to enjoy before you come traipsin'
back out here."

"It's just once every six months, Mr. Jones. I'll be
back in six months."

"Way they switch yall around up there ain't a
chanct in the world it'll be you but whoever it is
she'll know every one of them lowdown budgetin'
tricks. Worse than bein' in a straitjacket tryin' to git
by on the way yall figger up them budgets."

We talked about his budget. I was ready to leave; I
put my pencil in my bag, closed my notebook and got
up.

"No, ma'am, I don't reckon you'll git by that easy.
Now it looks to me like I'm in my rights to ast you a
few questions. What's all this about that old woman
gittin' her head bashed in? When I heared about it I
said, so hep us God, them thieves at the Bureau is be-
ginnin' to git what's comin' to 'em. Only murders I
ever knowed anythin' about or put real confidince in
has to do with love. Why, first murder I knowed about
I was about ten year old, not knee high to a grass-
hopper. Sam Wills found his wife makin' calf eyes at
some drummer. Let 'em both have it. Last murder I
heared about it was the same. I don't care how old
folks is let 'em get moanin' and groanin' about one
another and get 'em riled up or jealous and the first
axe they see or first shotgun they haul off and one of
'em looks like they been run through a sausage grinder.
Well, as for me I think a body ud ruther die thataway.

I ain't one that wants to sneak through life. By God, I want to be right in there rasslin', tusslin' and holdin' the bull by the horns right on up to the end."

I said good-bye. Mr. Jones started repeating himself. His words followed me through the rain to the street. "If I was one of them evermore lowdown scoundrel Nayzigh Germans yall couldn't treat me worser. Reckon yall don't mean no harm but it strikes me as the damndest most tom fool way in the world to be makin' a livin'."

CE CE CE

NIGHT came early, egged on by lashing winds. The waiting room was emptied of clients; Mr. Ricks, our persistent watchdog, always the last to leave, said good night to me as I passed him on his way out. I walked up the two flights of stairs to the third floor; the elevator had stopped running at five. From the other offices came the noises of those working late; even as I walked up the steps the sounds grew fewer. I heard steps in the first-floor hall, the front door banged shut, cutting off good-nights and good-byes and see-you-tomorrows.

Bea sat at her desk; around her, tacked on the partitions of her cubbyhole, Low's brilliant, biting cartoons were somehow cheerful. I was relieved to find Bea; the other stalls were empty. We decided to work an hour, then get some supper at the Frances Virginia and go home.

I sharpened pencils to fine points and then got a fresh supply of forms. They lay unused before me as I sat at the desk, going over the day; the inquiry; the visit to Mr. Lawrence; Mrs. Patch's funeral; the visit to Mr. Jones. All had drained me, leaving me without energy to do the work I had to do.

Twenty four hours previously Mrs. Patch had sat at her desk and now she lay in her new grave. As if to ignore her death I got up and walked to the window. The neon lights winked on and off. I had watched them the night before, I watched them now without seeing what they spelled out between blinks, what importunate messages they signaled to the world.

After a while I went back to my desk. The sharp point of the pencil snapped at the first entry I made in Mr. Jones's budget. I got up and peered around the partition to be sure Bea was still there.

Bea looked up and yawned. She smiled and threw her pen down. "This is no night to work," she said. "I've got a clothing order to get together. Then I'm ready to go. What about you?"

"I'm not accomplishing a thing. I can quit any time."

Bea went to the communal desk where we kept our key to the clothing-room; each division had a key to be used after hours when the room was closed. I listened as Bea walked down the hall; her first steps sounded loud, then I could barely hear them. I tried to detect the scratch of the key in the clothing-room lock, its turning, the opening of the door, but I couldn't. I thought again of Mrs. Patch alive last night, then dead last night, now in her grave; I wanted Bea to come back at once.

The wharf rat scurried in. He ignored my squeak and made his same general tour of the office.

I thought I heard someone move in the hall. The steps weren't Bea's; she moved quietly, but not that quietly. It was Bea, though, in the doorway. Instead of her own face she wore a death mask; her eyes were blind, she reached for a chair using her fingers tentatively, caressingly as a blind person does. She pushed her feet ahead of her in a way that suggested she might step into an abyss.

"What is it?" I asked. "Are you sick? What is it? Tell me. You're frightening me."

Her eyes didn't see me; her ears didn't hear; at last in a voice as dead as her face she said: "The clothing-room."

"What's happened? What are you trying to say about the clothing-room?"

Her lips trembled grotesquely; terror had taken her voice.

I ran down the long dark hall. Bea had left the light on in the clothing-room, cutting into the darkness. I rushed toward it and shoved the door back so that its knob banged against the wall. I saw what Bea had seen.

Mary was hanging dead from one of the clothing racks with a red pajama-cord around her throat. She bowed slightly like a shy little girl acknowledging applause at a recital.

I glanced around the large room, almost empty of

clothing, shelf after shelf bare, my eyes not wanting to see Mary again. I was doing anything to keep from seeing Mary. My eyes made an inventory of the clothing. The shelf in front of me marked Boys' Pajamas was empty. I counted three nightgowns on the shelf marked Girls' Nightgowns. I turned to look at the work table where the bundles were made up and wrapped, where the reports were typed. Then I saw a sheet of paper in the typewriter. I walked over and read it. I reached toward it to grab it and tear it to pieces; even as I grabbed I knew I must leave it. Those words were evidence.

I closed the door carefully and did not glance up to see Mary again. I turned the key in the lock and went back to the office.

Bea was crying. Her desk was dotted with crumpled blobs of paper handkerchiefs. The crying had released her so that she could talk.

"What must we do?" she said. "Suppose you hadn't been here. I don't know what I'd have done. I've been thinking what it must have been like last night when you were alone and found Mrs. Patch."

"Did you see the note—the one Mary left?"

Bea's eyes questioned me; she hesitated as if I had asked something too intimate to answer, then she said: "Yes, I saw it."

"I don't believe it. I don't believe it at all," I said. The words of the note left their engraving on my mind. I read them again: *When Jim died life ended for me. I don't want to live. My love to my mother*

*and everyone. Mrs. Patch's death was an accident. I
didn't mean to do it.*

"I don't believe it either," Bea said.

"But she said she did," I answered. "Why would
she say she killed Mrs. Patch if she didn't?"

In our disbelief and torment we shouted at each
other; then weariness owned us, crept in our voices,
made us ready to collapse.

At last I said: "We must let her mother know."

"I couldn't," Bea said. "I simply couldn't tell her."

I walked the obstacle course from Bea's desk to the
telephone. I lifted the great weight of the telephone
book and found Mrs. Lee's number; somehow I
dialed.

Mrs. Lee's voice, startlingly like Mary's, said hello.
At first I couldn't speak; Mrs. Lee's repeated hello
encouraged me.

"I don't know how to tell you, Mrs. Lee."

I told her who was talking; my incoherence seemed
to make sense to her; her voice comforted me.

"I've been expecting this," she said. "I'll miss her,
but I can't be sorry. It was death to watch her try to
live after she got that message about Jim. Every one at
the agency must have felt that. Now she'll have
peace."

There was more than that, the words lay nauseat-
ingly on my tongue. "Mary left a note. She sent you
her love and then she mentioned Mrs. Patch's death.
She said it was an accident."

Mrs. Lee didn't answer at once. I rushed into the silence and said: "We loved her, everyone here loved her."

Silence still shouted at me from the other end of the line.

"I imagine I should call the police," I said. "Will it be all right if I do?"

"Will you please, dear," Mrs. Lee said. "They'll have to be told. It will help me so much if you'll telephone them."

ᗕ   ᗕ   ᗕ

I TURNED to Bea when I had finished talking to Mrs. Lee. Her head lay on a stack of case records; she had lapsed again into shock. I found the number to call the police station. There was no excitement in the man's voice who answered; I gave directions how they could come up the back way; he said someone would be over soon.

"Say, that's where that woman was found murdered last night." He said it as a statement of no particular interest.

"Yes," I said.

"Okay, coming up."

Bea didn't respond to anything I said. I fished pieces of ice the size of grits from the water cooler and put them in a glass; then I dipped a handkerchief in the glass and wiped her forehead. The Atlanta remedy for anything is two aspirin tablets and a Coca-Cola; I gave Bea this standard medicine. She swallowed it and said thank you in a precise, strained way.

I thought of the previous night, the questions, the photographs. I began to coach Bea. "The police will be here. They'll ask us about everything."

We hadn't long to wait; soon the same man was back again calling me little lady. He said: "Well, little lady, you've had two tough sessions. First last night. Now tonight."

Bea was included as a little lady when I told him she had found Mary. Together we stood outside our office door and watched him make the long journey to the clothing-room; the other men followed him.

After a while the little-lady man walked toward us triumphantly, waving Mary's note. He beamed. "This clears up everything."

I told him I thought Mary's mother would want her body and he said: "Sure thing, little lady, we'll get in touch with her in a few minutes." He asked for Mrs. Lee's telephone number and said Bea and I could go.

Then I said irrelevantly: "Haven't I been followed?"

"Now, little lady, there are certain precautions we have to take. Nothing personal. You were the one who found Mrs. Patch. Anyway it's all over now and we didn't make it unpleasant for you."

He told us good night pleasantly and walked back to the clothing-room.

"I won't go," Bea said. "I won't leave Mary with those men."

I got her hat and coat and handed them to her.

"There's nothing we can do," I said. "I'll take you home."

I had trouble helping her downstairs; she kept wanting to go back. Outside on the street with the wind almost stripping our coats from us Bea walked better. We looked for a taxi and found one at last when we got to Five Points.

The driver scrambled out and helped me get Bea in the cab.

"Is your friend squiffed?" he said.

"She's had a terrible shock. Someone she loves has just died."

My remark made him abject; he got on all fours trying to make Bea comfortable. He wrapped a robe around her; he made her lie down.

"Sorry for what I said. I didn't know. Women are sure taking to drink these days. I thought I could suggest something that would bring her out of it if she needed it. But Hank can't work unless both feet are in his mouth. My wife says to me every day, she says, Hank keep that big trap of yours shut, but I never learn. I'm sure sorry for what I said."

I didn't think he wanted an answer, so I gave him none. I watched people rush for streetcars, then shiver and stamp their feet as they waited for the doors to open. A red light jolted me into a semblance of friendliness. I decided the driver might want an answer and I said: "That's all right. You were just trying to be helpful."

At the place where Bea lived the driver helped me

get her up three flights of stairs to her attic apartment.
I handed him some money.

"Look, I'm glad to do what I can, especially after
what I said. You don't need to give me all this."

Light from the third-story landing came just to our
feet; I couldn't see his face, I couldn't remember ever
seeing taxi drivers' faces, only the backs of their heads.

"Please keep it," I said. "And thank you."

I got Bea to the studio couch and poked pillows under her head. I turned on all the lights I could find.
I sat down, tired beyond belief. In a moment I looked
across the room in wonder; Mary smiled at me from a
corner. I had just seen her, with her head bent over,
her lovely hair falling in front of her face; now she was
restored, alive, her face full of compassion. I saw then
that it was a portrait Bea had done of her; a real portrait, Mary's essence was there. I couldn't help answering Mary's smile. I went toward it, pulled it
closer. I gasped. I said: "My God." Behind it Mrs.
Patch stared at me; her features had been flattered,
their grossness lessened, yet all her evil was apparent,
it pervaded the room. I looked again quickly at Mary
and let her portrait blot out Mrs. Patch.

Bea had turned toward the wall. I looked at her
slender back with awe. She saw too deeply and painted
too deeply, her brushes cut with insight and precision
into souls, nothing could hide itself from her large
blue eyes.

"You need something to eat," I said. She didn't
answer.

I went to the kitchen and fumbled around in the refrigerator. I made coffee and an omelet; there were enough greens for a salad.

She pushed the tray from me when I tried to hand it to her; I wasn't going to put up with her small child's tactics and I told her so. "I'm not going to spoon feed you," I said, using my own child's tactics. "You're not the only one. It's as bad for me. I loved Mary too. And I had to telephone her mother. I even telephoned the police."

My self-righteousness gushed out; the harpy near the surface took over. I handed her a fork and insisted that she eat. I took up a spoon and we ate from the same plate.

After our third cup of coffee we smiled a truce at each other.

"Go home," Bea said. "You need some rest. I've decided I want to work." She dragged out some tubes of oil paint. From somewhere she pulled out a large pad of drawing paper. She paid no attention to me and started to sketch. On the paper Mr. Ricks took form; three strokes made his face, four others his hurt, pathetic eyes, one or two his small twisted mouth. I looked at his soul for the first time: none of the qualities that sometimes provoked me were there, none of the suspicion, the tenacity, the cynicism; as Bea painted him I saw a magnificent little man whom life had treated harshly but whose courage and endurance and spirit were indomitable.

"Good night," I said.

"Good night," Bea said, "and thank you for all you've done."

On the way home I bought a paper. The world holocaust was back in the headlines, though Mrs. Patch was still on the front page. The piece about her said members of the Bureau staff had been questioned; no suspicion lay on anyone connected with the agency. In a few hours the morning paper would be out with later news. I discarded the paper, knowing the murderer, knowing the end of the mystery. Already I could see the headlines with Mary's name; I hated the thought of them; she had been all gentleness and kindness and now violence and death possessed her.

I was in my rooms, weariness rode on my back as I went about my chores. I swept the rugs and dusted picture frames. Suddenly a great tiredness held me in a knot; the terrible day came back, its awful moments dug at my brain: Mrs. Patch's funeral; Mary's death; I watched Mary dangle again in the air and make her small bow; I telephoned her mother the loathsome news.

Then my grim duty came to my mind. I telephoned Mrs. Martin and Peg. I decided after all that I would indulge myself; I asked Peg to let the others know about Mary. I threw a pillow on the floor near the fire; I turned out all the lights and lay down and cried.

⧵⧸ ⧵⧸ ⧵⧸

THE morning headlines were kind; they put
it as gently as possible. War Hero's Widow Commits
Suicide. Leaves Note Revealing Accidental Death of
Welfare Supervisor.

Mary's death touched everyone she had touched.
The waiting-room was filled with tearful, silent people, each hunched in his own despair. Even the elevator seemed to clank less heavily. No good-mornings
were said; we nodded at each other. Mary's desk
mocked the clutter in the rest of the office. It was clear;
she had planned her work so that it was finished before she died, the drawers were neat, the top of the
desk tidy with only the lamp and the desk calendar
on it. Our friend had left us, there was no comfort to
be had from one another, each of us sat alone grieving.

The clock moved slowly, the minutes clung to its
hands, holding them back. We did what work we
could; grief slowed us, made us the same in movement
and appearance, so that we all looked like one litter
born at the same time.

At twelve I went to see Mr. Lawrence. On my way
Mrs. Brown and Mrs. Williams, two of Mary's clients,
stopped me, their bodies bent and shortened by grief.

Mrs. Williams started to talk, her hands made hope-
less gestures of disbelief. "Why, Miss Mary was the
sweetest soul that God ever let live and that's the truth
and as long as I've got a tongue in my head I'll say
it. Then the radios started blarin' and the papers
comin' out that she killed that wicked old thang up

there that was nothin' but the devil's consort. They can print it and proclaim it till the second comin' of Christ but I guess I know she didn't have nothin' to do with it."

Mrs. Brown nodded and said: "Amen." Then she took up the lament in her high wailing voice. "Every word you're sayin', Mrs. Williams, is gospel truth." She turned to me. "Talkin' to you, Miss Wallace, I feel comfortible, talking to Miss Mary I felt blessed. You set with her a few minutes and, well, I don't know how to say it, she wasn't much of a one for words, the few she did say meant somethin', but as I was sayin' you set with her for a spell and when you got up you could stand up straight, you could draw a deep breath. I moved so's I could be in her district every time they changed you all up there at the Bureau. I couldn't a stood none of the rest of you all after havin' Miss Mary for my vizter."

They left me and walked on slowly, recalling to each other Mary's kindness.

"Why, Miz Williams, I remember when Will had the flu—" The wind took Mrs. Brown's comments; then flung some after me. "I don't know what we'll do. I can't imagine the Bureau without her. When Leander was born, why she—"

Soon I was at Mr. Lawrence's. On his porch I tried to lean my umbrella against a post. It tottered toward me and fell. I lunged to get it. Andrew was there before me, picking the umbrella up, steadying it, inviting me in.

From his mounds of pillows Mr. Lawrence smiled

and said: "How sad for you to lose such a friend as Mary."

"Yes," I said.

With cheerfulness that didn't seem out of place, he went on: "And so our murder mystery is cleared up almost as soon as it happened and we didn't get to solve it. It's just as well. Nobody likes an armchair detective, much less a bedridden one."

I said nothing. The clock ticked comfortingly; the coals in the fire seemed to chatter among themselves. After a while I heard Mr. Lawrence's soothing voice. "But you know, from what you told me I'd never have suspected Mary."

"The other day when we were talking about murder you said every one is capable of committing it."

"Yes, that's true. But Mary was involved in grief and hopelessness. It takes violent anger to do murder."

With tortured movements his crippled hands pulled the morning *Constitution* toward him and he read again the article about Mary. "I want to ask you about the note she left. You saw it?"

"Yes." I was reading it again. I was back in the clothing-room, seeing the note in the typewriter, not believing what I read.

Mr. Lawrence closed his eyes. "She wrote that and then hanged herself. That was her last act before the awful mechanics of killing herself."

I protested then as I had protested the night before. "But Bea and I didn't believe what the note said. We couldn't believe that Mary had killed Mrs. Patch.

We shouted at each other that she couldn't have done it."

"Tell me about last night," Mr. Lawrence's pleasant voice urged me. "Tell me about Bea finding Mary, then coming to you; what you did."

He listened quietly, encouragingly so that the night came back to me. I stood up and went to the hall. I used Mr. Lawrence's hall for the one leading to the clothing-room. I came into his room and it was the clothing-room; I dared not glance at the place where Mary's body was hanging. I was back with Bea, waiting for the police, I was making the telephone call again to Mrs. Lee, telling her of Mary's death. I was trying to get Bea home.

I dropped into the armchair exhausted.

Andrew brought us coffee and sandwiches. We ate, then Mr. Lawrence began to question me.

"You told me that on Monday Mrs. Patch made a scene over Mary's typing. Were there many mistakes in her suicide note?"

"Mary's typing wasn't as bad as Mrs. Patch pretended."

I hadn't answered his question; he was waiting for an answer. "No," I said, "there weren't any mistakes in the note Mary left."

He said nothing and I went on. "Don't you think at the last moment under the strain of what she was doing, with everything decided on, everything certain, she might have typed perfectly whether or not she was a good typist?"

"I suppose so."

Andrew came in with more coffee. Mr. Lawrence watched as I added cream, then said: "Mary was hanging there dead with a red pajama cord around her neck. You tried to keep from looking at her. And what did you do? You made an inventory of the clothing. You said a minute or two ago that no boys' pajamas were left. Yesterday when you told me about Mrs. Patch's murder and all the things that had happened at the Bureau this week you told me about an order for a little boy named Tommy Green. There was some discussion because the woman in the clothing-room didn't want to give him red pajamas. She said there were only two pairs left."

"I don't think I know what you mean."

"What I'm saying may not amount to anything. But I remember you said or I inferred that the cords are tied securely to the pajamas. All right. Mary used a red pajama cord to hang herself. She must have taken it from a pair of red pajamas. Yet there were no red pajamas when you went to the clothing-room."

I finished the coffee. My hand trembled as I set the cup in the saucer.

"You mean that someone came in and saw Mary hanging and still could get a clothing order together and leave without telling anyone what she saw?"

"But, my dear, remember how you felt when you found Mrs. Patch. You wanted to run away, to let someone else find her. Everyone wants to run away from unpleasantness."

"I wanted to run away. That's true. But I wouldn't

have had the composure to make up a clothing order."

"No. But with your friend hanging dead before you, you were able to see what clothes were on the shelves."

"I don't know what you're trying to say. Please go ahead and say it."

I looked into Mr. Lawrence's eyes; they were the kindest, most compassionate and yet most searching eyes I had ever seen. He said: "But I'm not sure. I need your help. Tell me again about Bea's reaction when she came back after seeing Mary in the clothing-room."

"She was stunned. Appalled. Shocked."

"Yet she's the girl to whom everything happens and she takes unusual things very well."

"Nothing that's ever happened to Bea compares with finding a dear friend hanging dead."

"Possibly not. But I think it was a great deal more than finding Mary dead."

He waited for me to say something as if a crucial scene had arrived in a play and he had given me my cue. I couldn't speak.

Mr. Lawrence made a suggestion. "Perhaps Bea knows Mary didn't kill Mrs. Patch."

"I told you we both said Mary couldn't have killed her."

"I mean I believe Bea knows who did kill her. I've told you I believe anyone is capable of murder. But once a murder is committed it has to have been done by a particular person. I believe Bea knows who killed Mrs. Patch. You told me about her painting—how she looks at the souls of people. She knows. She must know. And yet—" He shook his head, arguing with himself. "And yet— You said unaccountable things happen to Bea."

"Yes."

"Perhaps in some way Bea herself killed Mrs. Patch, not meaning to, and Mary knew it, so that when she committed suicide she left a note saying that Mrs. Patch's death was an accident, taking the blame for it."

"Mary would have taken the blame. Not just for Bea. For any one of us."

I was weary and confused; I didn't want to talk any longer of death and murder and suicide and blame. I looked out on the beauty of the winter garden, at the chrysanthemums holding up eager, bouncing heads in the boisterous wind; the quietness renewed me, gave me peace. Andrew entered and left with the tray, his movements like music, flowing into each other, their motifs love and service. I was ready to talk again.

"You can't know a person until you see him at the work he does best, can you?" Without waiting for an answer I kept on. "I thought of Bea as a kind of fall guy, a patsy, always getting herself needlessly involved, a bit inept, until last night when I saw those portraits. I've seen other things she's done. Peg has some in her house, but nothing like Mrs. Patch's portrait and Mary's and the sketch Bea did of Mr. Ricks. I saw something very close to greatness."

"Bea has been my favorite all along," Mr. Lawrence said. "You see, she's not afraid to make herself appear ridiculous. That's a rare quality. We're being ruined by fools who don't dare admit they're ridiculous."

We said good-bye then. He called me back when I was at the front door. "When you have time I think it might be interesting to check up on the pajama order and see which one of you made up an order while Mary was hanging dead in the clothing-room."

C⅃ C⅃ C⅃

Mrs. Sterling was at lunch when I went to the clothing-room. Mamie, her assistant, was busy at the typewriter.

"I hope I won't bother you," I said. "I want to check some orders made up yesterday."

Mamie looked up from a new hairdo. "I want you to know," she said, "that I didn't take all my lunch hour. I'm writing Herbert a letter. I don't write personal letters on agency time. I just couldn't wait to tell him about Mary. Just think, she was right over there."

I thumbed through the order file.

"My goodness," Mamie screeched, "you're the one who found her."

"No. Bea Shaw found her."

"But it distinctly says here—" She grabbed a stack of newspapers.

"Whatever it says, Bea found her. I came later."

Mamie read aloud: " 'Miss Beatrice Shaw, welfare worker, discovered Mrs. Allison's body.' Well, I'm sure it says somewhere that you did. Anyway you found Mrs. Patch. My goodness, after all you found her." Mamie moved away from me as if I might find her dead next.

She distracted me as much as I bothered her. I had to go through the orders again. Very little clothing had been given out; I found only one order for boys' pajamas, size ten, no color specified. That must be it, signed for by a cross mark. The name of the client who should have received the order was plain; the address was plain too, on Georgia Avenue, southeast. I wrote it down quickly.

I walked over to Pryor Street and took the Georgia Avenue-Grant Park car. At Capitol Avenue I got off and walked a short distance until I found the number I wanted; I beat against an open hall door. A little woman scurried out. When I told her what I wanted to know she shrieked; words charged out of her mouth in wild batallions.

"I was glad to do what I done. I signed with my cross, just like the vizter that come out with the pajamas said. I was proud to do it because them Watkinses needs whatever clothes you all will give 'em, they way they stink up this whole place. That's all I done, so hep me God, just signed the order with my cross and taken the pajamas. Just doin' my Christian duty, just tryin' to be neighborly, goin' to bed with as clean a conscience last night as anybody this side of heaven. And what happens? Here comes Miz Watkins yellin' at me in the middle of the night last night vowin' and declarin' that I stole the pajama cord, not thankin' me for seein' to her callers when she was out gallivantin' the Lord only knows where, though she says she was at the Grady."

I tried to soothe her, to stop the delirium of words. "Can you tell me who it was from the agency who brought the pajamas?"

"It was one of you all, that's all I know. You all look just alike and act alike, just peas in a pod, with them low heels and them hats and them black notebooks. I've saw her up there but I couldn't make no identification because I didn't have on my eye glasses, not that they woulda done no good because I've been needin' new ones and they's no way to git them out of you all up there. I really am put out by this here pajama order, to be called a thief by Miz Watkins when I was doin' her what I thought was a favor signin' my cross and takin' the pajamas, and now here you come trottin' out with all yore questions. I guess I'll find myself in a court of law on account of a pajama cord. I wouldn't put it past you or Miz Watkins to see I was sentenced to hard labor.

"Well, let's git the facks straight if I'm gonna be called to judgmint. Willie Watkins was took sick sudden. Here comes Miz Watkins acrost the hall beatin' on my door lowin' like a cow that's lost its calf. I done what I could while she just set and taken on. I called the city doctor and he called the Grady. Willie didn't have no pajamas to wear to the Grady and I didn't want him feelin' ashamed of hisself so I called you all, was after hours but one of you all answered. The operator said why that place is closed and I said go ahead and ring because somebody might be about, and sure enough after a while was this hello at the other end and I told her about Willie and she said it was after hours and she was busy but if it was a mergency she'd be right over with the pajamas. I said of course it was a mergency I wouldn't be standin' all shut up in that box at the drug store makin' no phone call and payin' out a perfekly good nickel if it wasn't a mergency and I'd thank her to git herself stirrin'. Here she come after a little while. I signed my cross and put on my hat and thought I was doin' a neighborly deed by gittin' on the car and goin' to Grady and takin' the pajamas. Certainly wasn't no treat for me havin' to go out in that rain and the Georgia Power Company didn't send no special car to take me I can tell you that. I waited and waited in all that rain for a car and then gittin' to Grady and astin' them people where to go and chasin' up and down them halls astin' this one and that one where I'd find Willie. Terekly I found him, throwin' up all over the place and his maw was cryin' so and takin' on so that I just laid the pajamas on the bed and come on back.

"Long about twelve, was just about to git myself settled to go to sleep here come Miz Watkins bangin' on my door astin' about a pajama cord. Reckon you lost it on the car she says, reckon I didn't I says, I guess I'm as careful as the next with property that don't belong to me, I wrapped it up with wrappin' paper used the last wrappin' paper I had, didn't want to use no newspaper, woulda come off on the pajamas. Tied it up with string, didn't use no granny knot neither.

Reckon you've come to the wrong place accusin' somebody of losin' somethin', I says."

Somewhere in the background I was vaguely con-
scious of another woman. Mrs. Simpkins had to stop
talking; her mouth's capacity to hold snuff had long
since been exhausted; she bent over the porch railing
and spit. The other woman leaned wearily against
the door. She began to speak calmly and slowly, yet
futilely, like a kind attendant trying to explain something to a psychotic patient.

"Now, Miz Simpkins, ain't nobody accusin' you of
nothin' and I'll thank you to lower your voice so's the
neighbors won't think we're rowin' and so's I can git
some sleep after settin' up with Willie all night long."

She looked at me as if I might be slightly less
psychotic than Mrs. Simpkins and might be able to
understand.

"Miz Simpkins was right nice makin' all them
phone calls, first to the city doctor and then to you all
at the Bureau. Tell you the truth I don't trust them
phones and can't seem to make no sense nor git no
sense out of them and I shorely appreciated all she
done. It was real nice of her to git on a streetcar late
at night and bring them pajamas to me at the hos-
pittle, a woman alone mighta been raped though I
don't see what temptation Miz Simpkins would be to
no man, black nor white. I shorely appreciated it. Was
just that the nurse said when she undone the bundle
ain't no pajama cord on one of these pairs of pajamas.
I said, I reckon it fell off and I'll ast Miz Simpkins
when I git home. So when I come home I merely ast

her what she done with it and she has carried on like
a sore tail cat ever since, chargin' up and down in the
hall like the fiends of hell was after her and yellin'
she won't be accused of things she ain't done. I tried
to pacify her and told her I guessed the cord was still
in the clothin' room and it really didn't make no difference as the nurse found out was plenty in one cord
to make two and she cut it and Willie is fixed fine as far
as pajamas goes, but they is just too many folks in this
world that the Lord shouldn't have give a tongue to."

"I just wanted to tell you," I said, "that we found
the cord. I'm sorry I couldn't bring it to you." I sank
into euphemism. "It's been used for something else.
I'm glad the nurse could make two out of one."

"You see," Mrs. Simpkins shrieked, "the Lord has
sent me a witness. Set yore trust in him and he will take
care of his lambs. I wrested with the devil all night
long and the devil's consorts and here is livin' proof
that I was with the righteous. I didn't lose no cord
because they wasn't no cord to lose. Oh, Miz Watkins,
you ought to git down on yore knees and beg my for-
giveness, you ought to fast and let nothin' tech yore
lips for forty days and forty nights for the lies you've
hurled and throwed and cast my way. It wouldn't surprise me none if the Blessed Redeemer didn't strike
you dead and make Willie a cripple for life for the
wicked things you've said to me."

I left Mrs. Watkins to the wrath of Mrs. Simpkins.

Mrs. Watkins fared better than I hoped. "Now,
Miz Simpkins," she said, as I went down the steps,
"you may just as well calm down. I ain't gonna pay no

more attention to you and if you pitch many more of
them fits of yourn they'll take you off to Milledgeville
in a straitjacket and I ain't the first one to say so."

⊄ ⊄ ⊄

WHEN I got back to the office Margy's husband
was pacing the floor in the disconsolate way men do
when they wait for someone. He was alone, his route
marked with milestones of crushed cigarettes. His
nervous hands had made a mess of his hair; his emotions seemed centered on his hat, which he twirled
and tugged and pulled.

I had planned to telephone Mr. Lawrence about the
pajama cord. The call could wait; Ted needed somebody to talk to; he was deeply troubled.

"Let's have a cigarette," I said.

Each of us in turn bowed toward the light Ted held
in his cupped hand; smoke circled around our heads,
giving a friendly, confidential atmosphere.

"Are things better?" I asked. "With Margy, I mean.
The other night you were awfully upset about her."

He drew on his cigarette as if he might draw an
answer from it.

"Look, Jane, you remember our talk after the party.
Well, I haven't told anyone. I wasn't going to tell anyone. But now that Mary's dead and everything is
cleared up I want to tell you. I did come here night
before last. About six or six thirty. I walked up to the

third floor using the back entrance just like you told me. I heard that woman's shrieking voice. I was so startled by the way she talked I didn't pay any attention to what she said. I just wanted to get out of here as quickly as I could. And I did. How did you all take it, day after day? No wonder Margy was about to crack up. I waited downstairs for a minute or two before I left. I don't know why exactly. I suppose I thought the poor girl who was taking all that might need a ride home or somebody to talk to. But nobody came down. When I left I swear the light was still on in Mrs. Patch's office. The papers said it was turned off when you went up. You didn't pass by me. You hadn't come by the time I left. I went on home. Margy wasn't there. She didn't come for a long time. She wouldn't tell me where she'd been. God, I thought everything. I've been worried crazy. I was in hell till Mary died and left the note. I thought Margy might have done it. After hearing Mrs. Patch I can understand how anyone could do it. Whatever that old girl got she deserved."

He unknotted his tie. He threw his cigarette to the floor. His hands made compulsive strokes through his hair.

The office filled with the other workers, back from having coffee. Ted left me and went to Margy's desk.

We all glanced into our compacts, even Miss Reeves; we made dabs at our faces with powder puffs, we made the ghoulish grimaces necessary to get lipstick on smooth. We poked around on our desks for small jobs, anything to postpone what we must do, anything to put off the sad, official farewell to Mary.

The time came. The church was packed with Mary's clients and friends. Bea and I found places together, the others went to the balcony. In front of us a woman whispered while her worn hands climbed up her hair to shove it under a battered hat, "Jesus is right now up in heaven tellin' her it was all right what she done to that woman, that is if she done it, which I doubt."

Above the somber whine of the organ we heard shoes squeaking and then Mr. Ricks's short, stooped body sauntered past us. He walked up the aisle and placed some chrysanthemums at the foot of Mary's coffin. Bea began to weep.

A man started to speak. I wished he would stop; there was no comfort in anything he said; the words came too easily to him and indifferently, like an actor grown stale in his part. I looked at the old men weeping and the old women, the blind; there was no need for the music and all those words.

At last we were outside. Peg said: "Nothing is as barbaric as a funeral. Why couldn't we just go alone and weep for her?"

No one spoke on the long ride back to Whitehall Street. We were glad to get back to the office; it was good to have work to do. For the first time in my life I enoyed the monotony of doing forms and budgets, revising face-sheets, getting lost in details.

About five we were dragged back to reality. The hall door opened.

Mr. Ricks rushed in and started to shout. "They's

never been nothin' so disgraceful and you all know it. Lettin' them git away with printin' in the paper that she kilt Mrs. Patch. Every last one of you up here knows it's a damned lie. And if you all don't do somethin' about it I'm gonna do somethin' about it. I reckon I could tell a thing or two if I had a mind to."

He slammed the door and was gone.

We looked at each other. We stared. I thought of Monday when Miss Reeves had yelled what everyone of us was thinking and hadn't the courage to say, that Mrs. Patch didn't deserve to live. Now Mr. Ricks had screamed that Mary couldn't do murder. And none of us denied it.

At five fifteen the telephone on my desk rang. I answered it wearily, hoping there was no emergency anywhere, I wasn't up to an emergency.

"This is Ellen Fitzpatrick." She said it in the tone she might use if she were on her way to be hanged.

"Yes, Miss Fitzpatrick," I said, and then listened to her sob.

"Please come out to see me when you can. I must talk to you. They're saying that dear girl killed my sister-in-law. She had nothing to do with it. Of course she couldn't have killed her. I've got to talk to you. I believe I know who murdered Jennifer."

Tact is for people very much in control of themselves. I had none left. I said: "I'm tired, so very tired. I'll try to come but I've got to finish up some work and eat first."

"Thank you, my dear. Thank you. Come whenever you can."

"I suppose it'll be about eight thirty or nine."

I hung up on her plaintive, abject thank you.

I said, not looking at anyone: "That was Miss Fitzpatrick saying that Mary didn't kill her sister-in-law. She said she thinks she knows who did."

No one answered me. No one said a word.

I picked up some cases and walked into the deep shadows of Mrs. Patch's office. I hadn't been in there in the dark since I found her dead. I turned on the light and she seemed to be there again. I saw her leaning over the records. They were spread out almost as she had left them. The case she had been reading was there: Charles Williams. I recognized the name. I looked again; it wasn't Charles Williams that I saw but Charles Wilson. Mrs. Martin had been in the office reading records and had left them to come back and finish.

The shadows confused me. I couldn't remember what I planned to do. I found myself at the general card file fingering through the W's. No Charles Williams was listed. I had certainly seen a case in that name on Mrs. Patch's desk; her dead hand had seemed to be reaching out for it. I went through the W's again, more seriously this time; there was no Charles Williams.

I hesitated to mention his name; then I was frightened to say it. I wondered if I dared ask a question with his name in it. My nerve came and went; I egged myself on; I went to the center of the office, midway between our stalls, and said loudly: "Which one of you has Charles Williams's case?"

Margy answered first. "Charles Williams? We must all have two or three cases with a name as common as that."

"Please look in your file boxes and see," I said.

The lids of the boxes on the desks squeaked open. I still stood in the center of the room like an irate teacher trying to get someone to confess to an offense. They all appeared to be obedient pupils, doing exactly as I asked, shuffling through their cards beginning with W.

Peg said: "I can give you John Williams and Joseph Williams. No Charles."

"I don't have any Williams cases at all," Gwen said.

"James and John G. are all I have," Bea said.

Miss Reeves couldn't oblige.

Smitty was amazed. "But I don't believe it. Not a single Charles Williams in all our hundreds of cases. Charles Williams ought to be nearly as common as John Smith. For fun let's see who has anyone named John Smith."

We looked at our cards. Bea was the only one who had a John Smith.

Margy said: "What is this, a game?"

"It's no game at all," I said. "Charles Williams's case happened to be the one Mrs. Patch was reviewing when she was murdered. At least it was on the top of the stack."

Peg said: "Maybe it's a closed case and will be downstairs in the closed files. Mrs. Martin probably approved the closing and sent it to files."

I decided to ask Mrs. Martin about the case. I walked downstairs to her office. Her desk was stacked with work, yet she had time for me or anyone who needed her. There was no sense of rush about her or anything she did, moments seemed to enlarge and extend themselves in her presence. I asked her about the case record. She thought a long time, at last she shook her head. "I don't remember—there were so many cases."

My face told her the disappointment I felt, though I said nothing.

"I see it means so much to you for me to remember. But I don't. I'm sorry." Her voice became easeful, placating. "Let me see. I think I sent all the cases from Mrs. Patch's desk back to the files. Let me go through these to be sure the Williams case didn't get mixed with them."

Her hands became the symbol of her. They were strong and beautiful, with short unpolished nails. The love with which she had used them all her life showed in every gesture; they threaded rhythmically through the stacks of cases.

"No, it isn't here," she said.

She pulled some work sheets out of her desk. "Let me go through these to see if his name is up for review this month." She riffled through the separate lists for the blind, dependent children, aged, and general relief. "It isn't on any of the lists. So that must mean that his case was either closed or for some reason it came up for a special review."

I thanked her and got up to leave.

Mrs. Martin said: "You're tired, Jane. Don't work any later tonight. You've had a terrible week."

"You're tired too."

"Then let's both go home. I'll straighten my desk now and leave. You ought to do the same."

There was no one in the office when I got back from talking with Mrs. Martin. I had wanted so much to know about the case of Charles Williams. And I had learned nothing. In the stubborn way in which one rushes after a train when it has already disappeared or runs to answer a telephone that has stopped ringing even as the key is in the front door, I went to each desk and thumbed through all the cards; not just the W's, but the whole alphabet. They had been right; no one had a Charles Williams. A thought skirted my brain, then left and came back again, this time boldly. Perhaps someone had torn up the card. I bent over wastebasket after wastebasket; every now and then I fitted together the puzzles made by torn paper; nothing yielded a trace of Charles Williams.

Nothing was working out; I had got in the middle of a fight when I tried to learn which worker took the pajamas to a client; Charles Williams didn't even exist and I was trying to make him important; soon I must go to the dismal house where Miss Fitzpatrick lived and listen to some dark suspicion.

I diagnosed my case: doldrums, depression. I prescribed for it: beer or wine drunk in some gay, cheerful place.

Finding a quiet place to drink alone wouldn't be

easy. After I searched for a while a place on Peachtree looked fine. The headwaiter said yes women without escorts were welcome.

In the half-darkness I followed him to a table. I ordered beer. I felt awkward alone; I made an inventory of everything in my bag. At last I ventured to raise my eyes; I read the legend on the match cover in the ashtray and inspected as if for flaws the design on the paper napkin. I was careful to look only at the table.

A man came up tentatively. I told him no thank you politely. In a few moments another man came up. I said no thank you again politely and pulled my glasses out of my bag. Another man came up. Just before I was about to congratulate myself that I was a femme fatale, glasses or not, I remembered that soldiers were the lonesomest race in the world.

A master of ceremonies told us where so and so had sung and what so and so had said about his singing and he knew we had a big treat in store. So and so came out, twisted a diamond ring he wore on his little finger, twisted his bow tie as if it were a handlebar mustache, looked lovingly into the spotlight, closed his eyes as he slid into the ether far, far above us, and sang *Dearly Beloved.* I wished very much that he would shut up and go away and let us all enjoy our drinks quietly. I was on my second beer before the thought ever seemed to occur to him.

Near me two women sat with their bodies hunched together; they were alert to each other's words but their eyes stayed on four soldiers who sat near by.

There was no direct invitation but somehow or other a nod was exchanged, there was a flurry, and the two women welcomed an ambush.

A major sat in lone splendor taking his time with his Scotch, eyeing each woman in the place in turn; the caliph deciding which hetæra to favor that evening.

Minor skirmishes were going on all around me.

I looked quietly into my beer and thought what an outrageous business sex really could be.

A private sitting alone got up and said: "Ladies and gentlemen of the Confederate States of America, I wish to make an announcement. God damn Southern women with their y'alling and their drawling. God damn Southern fried chicken. God damn Dixie."

Two waiters came and bundled him out of the place.

A cute honey child sitting near the private took her beautiful eyes off her escort, drank a long draft from her rum coke, and said with feeling to the quickly departing soldier: "Po' little ole homesick Yankee."

⊂⊃ ⊂⊃ ⊂⊃

I LEFT in the wake of the Dixie-damning private. As I crossed Peachtree to go in a restaurant I saw him hugging a lamppost and saying quietly, with committed earnestness: "God damn Robert E. Lee, God damn Jefferson Davis, God damn Stonewall Jackson,

God damn Jeb Stuart, God damn the Bonnie Blue Flag." Then he gave an ear-rending rebel yell and climbed halfway up the lamppost.

The beer made my dinner taste better than it had any right to. When I came out of the restaurant the Peachtree-19th Street car was waiting for a red light. I got on and asked the motorman to let me off at the right stop and then I began to look for the house.

"Relax, lady," the motorman said. "I'll let you know. It's a long way from here."

I relaxed. Traffic thinned out, lights became fewer.

A little later the motorman said: "I'll be dogged. I forgot. Your stop is two blocks back. Here, take a transfer."

"I'll walk," I said.

"I'm sure sorry, lady."

"Think nothing of it. Things like this always happen to me," I said and stepped off into a gutter.

His estimate had been on the conservative side; four blocks later I found Miss Fitzpatrick's house. I inched along the brick walk and stumbled up the front steps; the place was in darkness.

The door had been open when Peg and I went out; I supposed it would be open still; I tapped and pushed along the outside wall until I found the door. I shoved it and walked into the black cavern of the entrance; I groped trying to find a switch to the hall light; my fingers clawed against smooth surfaces.

I stumbled against a body. I screamed.

Something rushed at me from deep in the house, pushed against me, knocked me down. I felt something moist and sticky at my throat. I smiled and reached out my hand. "For heaven's sake, Joe or Bill —whichever one of you it is—stop it," I said.

There was another soft bound and both poodles yelped and began to lick my cheeks. We had a frenzied meeting, they lapped me, I patted them. I thought of matches in my pocketbook and scrambled in the morass of tissues, lipstick, change purse, notebook, keys. Bobby pins struck the floor; my compact tumbled and broke.

At last I found the matches. I lighted one; Bill and Joe barked and pranced, madly happy to see someone they knew. I turned and saw Miss Fitzpatrick lying on the floor. I went to her and called her name softly. I brushed her hair back from her face. The match burned my fingers; I threw it from me and struck another. Finally I found the switch but nothing happened when I pushed the button. I went back to Miss Fitzpatrick; she opened her eyes and said: "How nice of you to come," as if she were at the door saying: "Hello, do come in."

With the dogs superintending I helped her up. She sat down heavily on the bottom stair.

"I think the switch must be turned off," she said.

She and the dogs were blotted out in darkness as my last match flickered.

"You'll find the switch at the landing," she said. "Do be careful. I don't want you to fall down the stairs too. I fell down. I must have got my foot hung in the carpet. But then, there isn't a carpet. I really don't know what happened."

I found the switch; lights came on in the upstairs hall, the downstairs hall, and living-room.

Miss Fitzpatrick caressed Joe and Bill; they looked at her solicitously. She let me help her to a sofa in the living-room.

The bric-a-brac had been moved, the furniture placed neatly; restfulness had taken the place of clutter. On the marble-topped table stood a bottle of cheap domestic port, half empty, with a water glass near by stained in red. I noticed then that Miss Fitzpatrick had been drinking; the smell of port lay like a rich fragrance around her.

"You telephoned me to come. Do you remember?"

"Yes, I remember quite well. I wanted to talk to you about my sister-in-law. I wanted to tell you that I'm sure I must have killed her. But tonight something strange happened. I don't quite know what did happen. All day I've felt so guilty. Reading about Mrs. Allison—Mary. I didn't know her very well. I heard what her clients said about her at her funeral. She couldn't have done murder. Don't you know that? Never. She must have said she did it to take the blame on herself. I came home from her funeral. I couldn't get her off my mind. I telephoned you. I had to talk to you about everything. Then I started drinking. I had to get up my courage some way. Otherwise I couldn't betray my brother. He chose Jennifer for a wife, you know. To talk against her is to talk against him. But I must. I can't help it. I told you enough the other night for you to know how I hated her.

"I was sitting here drinking when the doorbell rang.

A very nice young woman was there and she asked me if I had rooms to rent. I told her yes. That friend of yours, that Mrs. Kelly, must have told her about them. By the way, I've rented two rooms to some people Mrs. Kelly must have sent out. They're moving in Monday. Well, I took this young lady upstairs to see the rooms. She said she liked them but she hoped to get a place with a kitchen. I told her she could use the kitchen downstairs whenever she wanted to. She thanked me and said she'd let me know and that I needn't let her out, she could find the way. I thought I heard the front door close. In a minute or two the lights went out in the hall. There's one switch for the upstairs hall and downstairs hall. I started down the steps. I know the house well and don't need a light. On the landing someone grabbed me. I don't know whether it was a man or a woman. A voice whispered: 'You silly old fool, stop telling people you know who killed your sister. You know quite well Mary did it. The case is closed. They'll think you're crazy—they'll lock you up if you don't stop talking that way.'

"I was terrified. 'Who are you?' I said. 'Who are you?' Whoever it was didn't answer. Then quite suddenly I was pushed and I tumbled down the steps."

I looked thankfully at the port. She'd had enough of it to make her relax; to break her fall.

"But that couldn't have happened," Miss Fitzpatrick said. "I must have imagined it. I must have had much more port than I thought. Who would want to hurt me?"

Her hands made fluttering designs of uncertainty.

"Of course that poor child Mary had nothing to do with Jennifer's death. I killed her. I tell you, I killed her. I did it with witchcraft. I really did. Here in the twentieth century. I made effigies of her. I stuck pins in them. I burned them. I shouted as they burned, die, die, die. Jennifer discovered me doing it one time. She laughed at me. She said I was a greater fool than she had imagined."

There was a frightened glint in Miss Fitzpatrick's eyes; the mellowness that the port had lent her disappeared.

"The witchcraft must have worked. You'll see why I had to kill her. No one else could have hated her as I did. None of you could have known her anger the way I did."

Her eyes remembered terrors too deep for tears; I couldn't look at her face.

"My brother and I were left alone as children when our parents died. We were separated and sent to boarding schools. We'd been left a great deal of money. From the time he was eight and I was seven we didn't have a home, then when we finished school we got an apartment together, later a house. My brother was the gentlest man who ever lived, the kindest, the most generous. Oh, it's true. It really is. And not because he was my brother. He met Jennifer. She was collecting funds for some agency. Somehow or other she got him to marry her. She destroyed him. He knew he was destroyed. One night he walked away. A few hours later what was left of him was picked up from the railroad tracks. Somehow she got all his money. There was nothing for me. I had no profession. No courage. I couldn't break away from her. She wouldn't have let me anyway. My misery was necessary to her. Then she married again. A man named Patch. He was a devil but kinder than Jennifer. He left her. I didn't ask questions. I haven't seen him since. The things I could tell you. I don't mean physical tortures, but tortures of the mind and soul—why once—"

I had listened too long. I had to stop her.

"But why do you say you killed her? You didn't."

"Because she's dead and someone must have killed her and no one could hate her as I did. You'd have to live with her twenty years as I have. You'd have to run when she called—you'd have to—"

"You don't need to tell me any more."

Her head rested on her knees; she sobbed.

Joe and Bill had listened quietly at the door; now they trotted over and stood close to her.

"Come home with me," I said. "I don't want to leave you alone."

"No, dear, I want to stay here."

"Let me call a doctor. You've had a bad fall. You may be hurt."

"No. I floated. It was like a dream. I'm not hurt."

"Then you must lock the house. You mustn't keep the front door unfastened."

Miss Fitzpatrick waited in the downstairs hall while I made a circuit of the house, locking windows and doors.

In her room upstairs she undressed and climbed into bed. I massaged her neck and shoulders and forehead. I told her about the soldier I'd seen earlier who wasn't very fond of the South; it was good to see her sorrowful face light up with smiles over his damns.

"Lock your bedroom door after me," I said. "And let Joe and Bill sleep in your room tonight."

"I'm so grateful," she said. "I can't tell you how kind you've been."

I said good night and waited outside her door to hear the key turn.

When I got to the head of the stairs she called to me. I went back and she spoke through the closed door.

"My dear, perhaps I didn't kill Jennifer after all. You may be right. I'm beginning to believe I didn't kill her. And I think I may be able to go to sleep now."

꘎ ꘎ ꘎

ALL the way home my mind was drugged with thoughts of Miss Fitzpatrick; the sad, pathetic days she had lived. The door to life had been slammed in her face; she had spent her existence in a dungeon, Mrs. Patch had been her jailer and torturer; her dreadful moments had eked away without friends or kindness or love.

I walked up the steep stairs leading to my rooms. I

reached for the doorknob, the faint light from the hall fell across the threshold.

My feet would not take me into the room, I dared not enter; somewhere in the dark was the end of my life. Beyond the door someone waited, the silence told me so, my trembling hands told me, the pain at my dry throat, my lungs that begged for breath.

I ran downstairs and out onto the sidewalk. I stumbled past darkened houses. I stopped and stood hard against a tree. Every now and then a car passed; its flight, its freedom of motion emphasized my aloneness. I circled the tree so that the car lights wouldn't shine on me; the wind dug at me malevolently; still I waited.

Above the tearing, beating, wailing sound of the wind I thought I heard a door close; I thought I heard careful footsteps. I might be watching someone, I might be only peering through the darkness at nothing; I thought I saw someone walk toward the corner and pause at the car stop. After a while a streetcar came and stopped, then started again.

I walked slowly back to the house where I lived. My feet insisted on going even more slowly up the stairs; I stood outside the door, then pushed it open. Just ahead of me was a lamp at one end of the couch. I turned it on. The room was empty; no one was in the kitchen, the bathroom and closets had no one in them. I called myself a fool as I stood shivering in the middle of the room.

Then I saw a cigarette burning in the fireplace. I stooped to pick it up; even as I touched it it became ash, a small mound of proof that someone had been in my rooms.

I reasoned with myself aloud while my teeth chattered. Someone had come for a visit, had waited, had left. A friend had been to see me. That was all. I must get on with what I had to do. I tried to iron; I burned a blouse; I tried to dust, a china pig leaped from my hand to the floor and shattered; I tried to read, words would not separate themselves, sentences had no meaning. I tried to go to bed and to sleep. There wasn't enough cover in the world to make me warm.

Sleep at last showed mercy, I dozed.

A sharp ringing woke me. I reached for the light and as the ringing went on I looked at the clock. Two thirty. That meant an emergency. Some child was hurt, some old person had a heart attack, a client had been put in jail, someone in my family far away was dying.

I grabbed a pencil and piece of paper to make notes. I said: "Hello."

A whisper, so gentle, so kind that I could barely hear it answered me. "Why are you afraid to come home at night? I waited and waited for you and then you ran from me. Why are you afraid of a friend?"

My hand could hardly hold the receiver, made slippery by the cold sweat from my palm.

I whispered too because my voice had left me. "Who is it? Who is talking?"

The whisper went on in its friendly, calm way. "Why don't you stop meddling in a case that's been closed by the police?"

CI CI CI

I GOT up. Death might have been whispering to me. I was cold beyond hope of warmth. I turned on all the lights; their brightness closed my eyes. Fatigue came and brought not sleep but some usurper that took sleep's place.

The wind bombarding the trees and windows waked me from fitful frightening dreams that had taken me to the edge of pits, up precipices, into dark traps of houses, among people determined to torture me, among people talking languages I couldn't understand, making demands of me in gibberish; everything and everybody colored in brilliant, terrifying shades of red, purple, orange, green, and a sickening blue.

Then the alarm boomed into my consciousness. I was more tired than I had ever been, the cover pressed down on me, adding to the weights I couldn't lift of fatigue and fear. I didn't want to go out in the world, the small part of the troubled world that Atlanta was. I didn't want to look on hungry people, to visit in their homes, to smell the deadly smell of poverty and to escape from it so easily, by the simple gesture of closing a door. I had no relish for the agency where a murderer went about her daily routine and took time off at night to frighten Miss Fitzpatrick and to terrify me. I didn't want to face the workers, to look at each one to try to see if she acted like a murderer. Whoever it was was someone I gave a Christmas present to, someone I shopped with, wished well, loved, exchanged confidences with, and borrowed money from if payday was too far off and she happened to have enough change to spare.

But I had no choice. I must leave my rooms. Somehow I got through the trivia of coffee-making and dressing. Somehow I found myself in my district. I made five visits and at one o'clock went to the office; no one was there. I got a Coca-Cola from the machine and sat at my desk drinking it. Everything seemed peaceful, the stalls looked the same, wastebaskets were full of paper, the desks littered with mail and case records, lamps were crooked narcissistically as if they gazed fondly on their reflections in the desk tops. Margy and Gwen wore smocks when they worked, and these were folded neatly on the backs of their chairs. I called myself an imbecile to be afraid.

My mail had stacked up. The pigeonhole with my name on it was stuffed; I reached for the letters and requests, so earnest and defenseless. Some of them had been addressed to other agencies in the hope that those agencies might give assistance that we couldn't; some were directed confidently to the President of the United States, some to his wife; but no matter where they were sent, all the letters found their way back to us.

The tops of the letters had been penciled in by the mail clerk with the case names and numbers. The first one I picked up was marked in red Kannon, Mollie A., case number 107-1091-A.

Honey, now do send me them clothes. You know I need them or I wouldn't be asting for them. I aint one of them scroungers that asts just to hear their voice or writes just to see what their handwriting looks like. I pray for you and your friends every night and ast God through his precious son Jesus Christ to save you from your sins and to pertek you from your enmies.

Next was a short note written on a paper sack.

Mis Walis, I will sure thank you to get down here as soon as you can and give Pete a good talking to. He is going up and down the street swearing and declaring that he aint Minnie Mae's father and he aint Joe Lee's father when he knows good and well he is and I have got two witnisses to prove it.

I picked up a postcard with a simple request.

I want some clothes. I want some rent. I want a grocery order. I want some attention. I want everything up there that they is to be had for nothing.

Mrs. Ada Smithson wrote discursively.

I am sending my close order and I have herd they was giving matries again if they are—will you order me one for the boys bed a full size and one for the girls a 3 quarter for there beds is tore all to peaces and I told you we was trying to trade the old man's pistel and watch for and old car or mule & wagon for him to go in for looks like he will

*get a past going sometime and maybe if he had
some way he could hold out he could do some
peddlin so his daughter that is dead her husband
lent him money to get an old car and said we
could pay him as we could I told him if we
couldn't pay for it we could let him have it back
and I sure do thank you for the 5 dollars you sent
me for rent. I cant hardly go with my kidneys is
geting back again and my feet hurts so bad I
have to soak them when I get home ever time
I go out. Annie Lee has been out again several
nights till way past bedtime and she seems to be
gaining weight I am sorry I told her better but
I guess talking aint no way to discouradge nobody
from doing that when they got their mind set on
it so you better add to the close order some infer-
ent clothes for she will be gneading them soon I
am afraid. Don't it beat all the way things can
happen I cant never tell whether I ought to be
crying my eyes out or dying laughing.*

The wobbly penciled letters showed the travail Mr.
Will Adams had suffered in writing the next letter
in the stack.

*When you was out here last week I told you I
was writing some poetry and you read what I
had wrote. Well, the other day right after church
the Lord God revealed hisself to me. I just fell
right there in the isle and blessed his holy name.
Preacher come up when I come out of it and said
was a revelation if ever he seen one. Sure enough*

*I was give a sign. I believe I told you how I hum
and haw over writing down my poetry. Well,
wasn't no humming and hawing about this. I just
set down, told my wife to wait dinner a few min-
its and this poem come to me like the ten com-
mandimints come to Moses straight from God
all in one big swish and flash. Here it is. I aim to
have it printed and sell it for ten sints a copy of
course you are sure welcome to it wouldnt think
of charging you one red penny for it.*

Moan, sinner and fall on your knees
Its not yourself its Jesus you must please
Foam at the mouth sinner
Your guts will burn in hell
Because the straight and narrow you didnt follow
*   so well.*
Writhe sinner, the devil will whup you
With his tail
Because our sweet Lord Saviour you did fail

THE END

*Revealed to old man Will Adams follering
protaked meeting conducted by Brother Jim
Watkins*

A note on scratch paper fell to my lap. I read it; my
eyes refused to send the message to my brain. I read it
again.

*Why don't you stop your silly suspicions about
Mrs. Patch's murder?*

I looked at the neat printing in pencil, the delicate blue of the paper; at the back of my neck nerves and muscles twitched, I had a strange sensation that I was being lifted and shaken. My hands trembled; the letters fell from my desk to the floor. The Coke bottle wavered and plunged, then twirled around and around on the floor as if invisible hands played Spin the Bottle; Coca-Cola gurgled out of it like blood from the throat of a dying person.

        ⊂⊐   ⊂⊐   ⊂⊐

I HAD a desperate need to be near someone. I must have something to warm me. I went across the street for coffee. On the way I passed by the waiting-room; the voices rose and fell, I distinguished no words, I looked for someone I knew, I wanted to greet another human being; all the faces seemed to turn from me. Cold and terror owned me. My hand still clutched the printed note. My neck was stiff from the tension of fear.

Eddie sprawled against the counter and nodded when I asked him for coffee.

"Too bad this ain't a bar," Eddie said. "You look like you could use a drink."

I didn't dilute the transparent coffee with milk. I pulled the cup toward my mouth with both hands. Even then I couldn't hold it steady; a stream spilled on my coat. I tried mopping it up with a paper napkin, which left bits of fluff in the nap of the wool.

Eddie and I had no small talk for each other. With others around us we could speak intimately of people, tease about appearances, make jokes about his place of business, about our agency. Alone we were struck dumb by eath other's strangeness. We were embarrassed by the silence. I tried to hide my uneasiness by concentrating on the coffee, making an engrossing job of sipping it, stirring it, while Eddie flapped around with a wet cloth on the counter.

Maybe it was the way I looked, maybe it was the silence Eddie couldn't take any longer. Anyway he said: "God, but you look awful. If you'd been dug up you couldn't look no worse."

I didn't try to answer him. Nothing steadied me. The coffee did no good, walking across the street hadn't helped. I didn't want to go back to the agency. I loitered over the last drops of coffee, now cold and bitter. At last I handed Eddie a dime. The nickel change dropped to the floor. I was grateful for Eddie's and my scramble underneath the cigarette counter, pawing around for the nickel; anything to put off going back to the office.

Downstairs at the Bureau I looked in again at the waiting-room; I was still ignored; no one paid any attention to me. I missed the elevator and was glad; it crawled back. All my excuses were used up, there was no way to put off getting back to work.

The office was exactly as I had left it, still empty. I cleaned up the coke that had spilled on the floor and went back to work. Darkness came at a few minutes after four. I looked out in the blackness and a thought tugged for remembrance, as if I had put something down, meaning to pick it up, and had forgotten. I filled out some forms and checked them again and again because my mind wasn't on them but out somewhere trying to uncover and search out what it was hunting. I shoved the stack of records away from me and there, in their place, was the thought, almost embodied, almost able to speak.

Mr. Ricks hadn't been in all day.

He hadn't missed a single day since the agency opened. He was our Cerberus, our keeper, our jailer; day after day he watched us with his small all-seeing eyes; he sized up our actions with his sharp, agile brain.

I telephoned the receptionist. "He must be around some place," she said. "Nothing could make him miss. He had flu up here last winter. I couldn't make him go home even then until closing time. Come to think of it I don't remember seeing him today."

Her alarm matched mine. She said anxiously: "I hope nothing has happened to him."

I scratched *Visiting—Will Not Return* on a piece of paper. I anchored it down on my desk with a chipped, battered donkey paperweight and left.

When I got to Crew Street Mrs. Cole, Mr. Ricks's landlady, nearly choked herself in her eagerness to talk.

She jerked me into her bedroom and shoved me into a chair by the fire. The mantel was posted with a huge sampler warning Be Sure Your Sins Will Find You Out, and a calendar for 1926 with a picture on it of a distraught, terrified person, enveloped in great waves, grabbing at a stone cross, and underneath the cross was the legend Rock of Ages Cleft For Me. The mantelpiece itself was bare except for a glass of water full of a detached, disembodied grin made by Mrs. Cole's false teeth.

Mrs. Cole started to talk. She decided that her speech was too full of hisses and reached for her teeth. She poked them in her mouth as if she would swallow them; she made a few adjustments with her tongue, then started her story all over again.

"Well, now, honey, you may well have missed Mr. Ricks today seein' as how he didn't go up there and he couldn't go up there, bein' the first time he has ever failed to go up there. Was last night, he didn't come home and he didn't come home and I said, law, that ain't like Mr. Ricks. Bill says he can set his watch by Mr. Rickses comins and goins, and I says, well, what do you suppose has happened to him, as long as he's lived in this house he's been home and in bed by eight of an evenin'. He stays up there at the Bureau until you all close and goes on over to the lunchroom on Decatur Street for his supper, then comes on here. Somethin' bad musta happened, I says to Bill, they's so much meanness goin' on we oughta check up, so Bill he goes on down the street and asts Mr. Green if he can use his phone. So Bill he calls the manager of the National and he says Mr. Ricks ain't been in for his supper. All this seemed mighty peculiar to Bill for

Mr. Ricks is a mighty methodical man, nobody like him for doin' the same thing at the same time day in and day out, no need for me to tell you that, anybody at the Bureau knows that, so Bill he decides to do as much checkin' as he can and he walks on up Pulliam to Rawson till he hits Pryor then to the Bureau on Whitehall. Wasn't a sign of Mr. Ricks. If it had a been summer Bill coulda checked up by people settin' on their porch but nobody wasn't settin' out in all that miserable weather. No, wasn't nobody that had saw hide nor hair of Mr. Ricks.

"Bill come on home and I says when things git to this fix ain't but one thing to do and that's to call Grady and Bill he called. Well, they was a lot of hummin' and hawin' and callin' back and forth and gittin' a different one and sayin' we can't give that information on the phone, so Bill he just goes on over there and long about eleven he come back and says Mr. Ricks had been picked up on a corner, I believe it was Pulliam and Woodward, looked like a hit and run driver had got him, or maybe he'd just fell in a fit, wasn't no car marks on him, anyways he was out of his head, though they was all hopin' they wasn't nothin' serious wrong.

"Today Bill he went back over there durin' visitin' hours but they wouldn't let him in to see Mr. Ricks. Bill could hear him railin' and rantin' though sayin' he was gonna git every woman up there at the Bureau if it was the last thing he done."

I listened to Mrs. Cole repeat the story with minor variations and enlargements three times and said I must go; I could tell she thought me an ingrate not to listen at least once more.

At the corner drug store I stopped and telephoned a social worker at Grady Hospital. She asked me to wait. In a few minutes she came back with a report; yes, Mr. Ricks had been brought in the night before, about six. Someone had called and the ambulance had gone out. There was no evidence of a hit-and-run driver. He might have fallen and injured his head. He was in good condition. The doctors wanted him to rest for two or three days. He wasn't talking much; when he did talk he repeated the same thing. Mrs. Cole, the landlady, had censored what her husband had overheard Mr. Ricks say. Whenever he did say anything in the hospital Mr. Ricks said he'd get every single one of them whores of Babylon up at the Bu- bureau if it was the last thing he ever done.

⊂⊨ ⊂⊨ ⊂⊨

At Grady a nurse pointed the way to Mr. Ricks's ward.

I walked past the beds until I found him. He looked smaller than ever, swaddled in the sheet in the high, narrow bed.

He played possum, not answering when I spoke to him, and I glanced across the ward filled with per- sons, some convalescent, sitting up, bored with the tedium of illness; others strangled by pain, finding each new stab a surprise of horror.

After a while Mr. Ricks looked at me. He wouldn't speak.

"I'm sorry you're in the hospital," I said.

He turned away from me. "You bein' sorry ain't heppin' me none."

"Please tell me what happened."

He still didn't move toward me. His face was muffled in a pillow. "Ain't much to tell. Can't make much of a story out of it. One of you all up there at the Bureau pushed me. That's the long and short of it."

"Why do you say that?"

He sat up very straight as if my stupid question jarred him beyond endurance. "Whoever kilt that Miz Patch pushed me. A man old like me, not doin' no harm to nobody."

"The papers said Mary Allison killed Mrs. Patch. And Mary's dead."

Mr. Ricks groaned at my imbecility. "You know as good as I do Miss Mary never kilt her. She couldn't a kilt nobody." Thinking of Mary he stopped talking; his eyes shone at his brain's reverie. "Talkin' to Miss Mary was like goin' to yore mother when you'd been hurt real bad. She was like a breeze comes to you finely in the hot summer when you're near dead from heat. And them papers sayin' she kilt that woman. Why she wouldn't a tetched that old Miz Patch. And when I up and told you all that she didn't when you all come in after Miss Mary's funeral, well one of you all waylaid me, that's what you done, and here I lay, just because I told the God's truth. Minute I git outa here I'm goin' right back up there and say it again. Miss Mary didn't do it."

He turned his back to me again. I was his enemy.

"I don't think Mary did it either," I said.

He looked at me and accepted me for the first time since I'd known him. He smiled a baby's toothless smile and stretched his legs.

"First word a sense I've heared you utter since you been at the Bureau."

"Do you have any idea who killed Mrs. Patch? You keep pretty close check on us, Mr. Ricks."

"I don't mean nobody no harm by it. Only place I got to go is up there. Can't read. Don't do no good to go to the liberry. Ain't no sense settin' in the liberry turnin' them pages up there lookin' at pictures I can't tell who they air or what they air."

"I just meant that maybe you saw something or have an idea who killed Mrs. Patch."

"Of course I never seen nothin'. Of course I ain't got no idear. I ain't a man that would hinder the law. If I'd a knowed I'd a told straight off."

A man next to Mr. Ricks groaned for water; no nurse was near. I started around Mr. Ricks's bed but he was out and handing a glass of water to the man before I could get there.

The antiseptic smell in the ward stifled me. I looked out of the window against which the winter wind rattled. Mr. Ricks scrambled back in bed and suddenly clasped at his head as if he had forgotten his own pain in the greater need of the man next to him. His face wore the distortions of agony; it was stupid, needless. I thought of the night before, Mr. Ricks walking home slowly, following his usual route, not deviating, satisfying some need of his soul by following his precise path day after day, night after night, and being knocked down by someone waiting for him because he had spoken of Mary with love and had said she couldn't do murder.

I wanted to embrace him; I couldn't tell him what I felt. Instead I asked: "Is there anything you want or need?"

"No, ma'am, thank you."

"I'd like to bring you anything you want or if you have a message for your landlady I'll be glad to give it to her."

"Well, to tell you the truth I could use a little chewin' tobakker."

"I'll be right back with it."

"Tomorrow'll be plenty soon. I don't want to put you out none, don't want to be no trouble to nobody."

I walked downstairs and out through the entrance to the street, on down to some small stores on Edgewood. The man who sold me the tobacco made a feeble joke about women chewing these days, doing everything these days, yes, sirree. I tried to smile. We both tried to smile at his joke.

Mr. Ricks was dozing when I got back to the hospital. I put the tobacco on his pillow and left.

Downstairs in the lobby a woman walked slowly toward a man standing in front of a window. Her hand guided him around to face her. She leaned close to him, her nose touched a button that dangled from his coat. "He's dead, my darling," she whispered. "He's dead. Our son is dead."

I walked out of the hospital into the tomb coldness of the night.

⊂⊃　⊂⊃　⊂⊃

I WENT to a small blight of a café near the hospital. From the dog-eared months-old menu I asked for Today's Special.

The food wouldn't go down. I paid my check. The waitress followed me asking if I wanted something else, she was sorry I didn't like what I had ordered. I thanked her and told her the food was all right, I just wasn't hungry, that I had enjoyed the coffee a lot.

Outside in the wind I thought of Mr. Ricks, of the man and woman facing the new sad fact of their son's death; I had walked out so easily on all that sorrow.

I had to talk to someone. The thought of Mr. Lawrence flooded my mind like a benediction; he would listen to everything I had to say; I felt I must see him at once. I spoiled myself and took a taxi to his house.

I knocked on the door; there was no answer; I knocked again, louder. Still Andrew didn't come. I pounded on the door, in terror that this final haven had somehow been snatched from me. At last Andrew opened the door and begged my pardon for keeping me waiting.

In Mr. Lawrence's room the night enclosed us; there was a comforting silence, disturbed only by the sifting of the coals and the neat tick of the clock disposing of the minutes. The fire held me in hypnosis. Andrew hadn't turned on the lamps; the fire gave a gentle, soothing light; I was rested by the room; Mr. Lawrence's presence encouraged me to say what I had to say.

My speech jumped back and forth; I told him about the pajama cord, Mary's funeral, going to see Miss Fitzpatrick, a hodgepodge of words. I told of leaving Mr. Ricks only a few minutes before. Mr. Lawrence asked no questions; I went back over the incidents; his attention encouraged me to recall everything. Finally the torrent of words ended.

After a while his voice came from the shadows of the bed.

"Tell me," he said, "has all this cloyed your appetite for murder stories?" For a moment the question seemed strange, then I realized that it was better than any comment he might have made on what I had been saying.

"No. Not at all. That is, not for detective stories. I'm not so sure I want to read about actual crimes just now. Too many people go unpunished."

"But none of us gets the punishment or reward he deserves."

"Maybe that's why I want it to happen in what I read."

We didn't speak again until Andrew entered and turned on the lights. I watched him stand at each lamp and turn it on, the circle of light illuminating the even beauty of his calm features.

Mr. Lawrence blinked against the lights and looked at me a long time. "This isn't polite, my dear," he said. "But how tired you look. And tense. I'm afraid the week has been too much for you. Andrew, I believe you can help."

Andrew came to my chair; his strong, friendly hands were at the back of my neck, massaging, kneading, rubbing away tension. The tiredness was gone. I wanted to clasp Andrew's hands, to embrace them for their kindness; all I did was to thank Andrew very much.

He left the room.

"That's twice today I've wanted to embrace someone," I said. "Mr. Ricks and now Andrew. I wonder why I couldn't."

"The important thing is the love you have for Mr. Ricks and Andrew."

I didn't answer; Mr. Lawrence edged away from intimate talk. He said: "I gave out of detective stories last night. Today I've had to content myself with other kinds of books. I couldn't have picked a more exciting story. It had to do with murder. Perhaps that's why it interested me so much. 'The Pardoner's Tale.' Its theme, you remember, is that avarice is the root of all evil. Lust for money. Lust for material things. I read it with a sense of discovery, as something very personal. I somehow felt sure it would help us.

Now wouldn't it be ironical if it's Chaucer and not Dorothy Sayers or Ellery Queen or Conan Doyle or any of the other mystery writers we admire who will solve our murder for us?"

Avarice seemed an extravagant, inappropriate word to apply to any of us at the agency; I told Mr. Lawrence so.

"But how do you know? Who really knows anyone? Anyway, we must consider everything. Now then, can the murder involve money? Can any one be taking money from the Bureau?"

"I don't see how. The checks are sent to the clients. We don't even see the checks. Anyway who needs money enough to steal it?"

"Please go along with me. Think of all the workers, not those in the entire agency, just those in your section. Who needs money most?"

"Margy, I suppose. She has three children. One of them is sick a great deal. Her husband works but I don't think he makes much."

"What about Miss Reeves? Doesn't she have an invalid mother? Wouldn't that take a lot of money?"

"I don't really know. From what Peg said I don't think Mrs. Reeves has a doctor. Her pains aren't the kind that can be treated by medicine."

"Gwen?"

"She doesn't need money. She had a deposit slip for eight hundred dollars on her desk Monday."

"Bea?"

"Money is nothing to her."

"What about Peg and Smitty?"

"They never mention money."

"Perhaps Chaucer can't help us after all. Now, I want you to tell me again everything that has happened since you were here—the visit to your room, the telephone call later, the note you found today."

I told him again, watching his face take on the look of unbelief, disbelief, abhorrence, pity, compassion, terror, tenderness.

"Do you know why you've been threatened?"

"Because I don't believe Mary killed Mrs. Patch."

"But none of the workers believe it. I think you're being threatened because you're the only one who is doing anything about it. Look what happened to Miss Fitzpatrick. She got a nasty push. Look at Mr. Ricks. He was shoved. You three have shown that you don't believe Mary killed Mrs. Patch. The other workers know Mary didn't kill Mrs. Patch but they aren't doing anything about it."

"I'm not doing anything about it."

"Yes, but you are. You weren't really a threat until you mentioned the case of Charles Williams."

"But the case of Charles Williams doesn't exist. I've looked in every card box. I've asked everybody. No one has the case."

"I repeat, you weren't a threat until you mentioned the case of Charles Williams."

"But that's silly. Suppose I find the case. If it's Old Age Assistance there'll be nothing in it but an application, proof of age, a budget sheet, some forms, copies of clothing orders, and a narrative telling about home visits. If it's a Blind case, or Dependent Children, or

General Relief the same kind of information will be in it."

It was nine; I felt I had to leave. I dragged myself up from the chair and put on my coat, dawdling, making the task last as long as I could.

"You'll try to find Charles Williams's case tomorrow, won't you?" Mr. Lawrence said.

"Yes, I'll go to the closed files and see if it's there."

"You're tired. And you were tired when you came. But I think you notice things and I'd like to check on something. When you came tonight did anything seem unusual?"

"No, I didn't notice anything out of the ordinary."

"But think."

My hand brushed my tired forehead. "No, I don't remember anything."

"All right. I'll give you a hint. It had to do with Andrew."

"It seemed to take him longer than usual to answer the door. I don't remember ever waiting so long for him to come. I was tired, though. Maybe it only seemed longer."

"It was longer. And you noticed. Good. Nothing really gets by you. Why should it take longer tonight?"

"Perhaps he didn't hear me. Maybe he was busy."

"He was busy. Putting something away—something you told me about. You see, I'm working trying to catch up with you."

"I don't understand."

"I won't bother you about it tonight—it may not be anything."

Mr. Lawrence wouldn't tell me more; we said good night.

Andrew insisted on going with me to the car stop. I walked quietly beside him; we did not speak; his strong body sheltered me from the wind. The streetcar came; we said good-bye. Andrew waited until the car went past; through the blurred window I nodded to him, he answered with a wave. I watched him turn and walk back toward Mr. Lawrence's house.

When I got home I was too tired to be frightened; I was too weary to wash my pants and stockings; I stuck them in a laundry bag. I did a half-hearted job of rolling up my hair; I sat in the bathtub without scrubbing myself. When I finished bathing I went over to the shelves for a book, wanting one that had never failed me. I glanced at *The Circular Staircase*, *The Confidential Agent*, *Fer-de-Lance*, *The Listening House*, *The Eyes of Max Carrados*. *The Beckoning Fair One* seemed the most inviting; I took it to bed.

The telephone rang; remembering the last call I had I dropped the book. I wouldn't answer. I didn't want any more whispers, any more kind, gentle threats. The ringing stopped. I found my place and started reading again. The telephone rang; there was no denying its insistence this time.

It was Peg. "Reading penny dreadfuls as usual?"

"Well, I'm reading *The Beckoning Fair One*. What are you doing?"

"I'm reading too. *Miss Lonelyhearts*. The man is amazing. Nathanael West, I mean. The book is so

short, yet everything is in it. Defeat. Terror. The
negation of living. It's about a man who writes advice
to the lovelorn. You should read the letters people
write him. Listen."

She read one, something hideous about a young girl
who had no nose; another about a deaf and dumb
adolescent girl who had been attacked. It wasn't like
Peg to talk on the telephone so long; she had the rare
faculty of saying what she wanted to say and hanging
up.

"What's the matter, Peg?"

"What do you mean?"

"All this about Nathanael West. What is it?"

She hesitated; then she said: "I'm frightened."

"Why?"

"I don't know. When we drank coffee this afternoon
everything seemed strange. Nobody talked. Eddie
asked what was wrong. He said we looked like the
grand jury was hiding under the table making an investigation. He said you'd been in about an hour earlier and acted like your own ghost. I just felt uneasy
about you. I wanted to find out if you were all right."

"I'm fine. Just very tired."

Still Peg didn't say good-bye.

I said: "Do you want to talk about Mrs. Patch's
murder?"

"No. Nobody at the office does. We all avoid it. We
don't dare mention Mrs. Patch and we don't dare
mention Mary."

Again there was a long silence; at last Peg said good
night.

I had barely hung up when the telephone rang again. It was Mrs. Martin, sorry to bother me but Amelia Betts in her division had pleurisy. She'd made all her visits but hadn't dictated them; nobody could read her notes, so everyone was taking an extra review. Mrs. Martin gave me the name and address of the person whose review had been assigned to me; the client lived in the northwest section. The deadline was noon next day.

We said good night. Once more I picked up the book; I finished it and was caught up in its horrible end, Elsie Bengough was on her way to the morgue; Paul Oleron was on his way to prison, not aware of the tragedy that his strange, obsessive love for the haunting, ghostly Fair One had caused. I wondered if people hovered on after death as the beautiful woman had stayed on all those years to haunt the room of Paul Oleron; I wondered if Mrs. Patch still divided her time between her house and the office. I put *The Beckoning Fair One* back in its place on the shelves; I couldn't set aside its spell.

To try to quieten myself I thought of what I must do the next day. I looked at the name and address I had written down when Mrs. Martin telephoned; I had to review the case of Mrs. Mary Walters the very first thing.

After that I must search again for the record of Charles Williams.

⊂╪ ⊂╪ ⊂╪

MRS. WALTERS's front door rattled under my knock, the loose knob wobbled.

A woman next door came out to chide me. "Ain't no use you tryin' to beat the door down. Ain't a bit a sense in it. Miz Walters ain't home. Went to town to pay her gas bill. She'll be home tereckly. You might as well go and come again or set still and hold yore peace."

I sat on the prickly, splintered steps to wait and shivered as the wind struck me.

At eleven Mrs. Walters came. When she saw me she backed away like a photographer getting the right angle. She closed her eyes and nodded, satisfied that she had it. She motioned me to follow her into the house. We entered her bedroom; family portraits hung from high on the walls on elaborate tasseled cords, a brush broom leaned against the grate, there was a center table swathed in crochet, the bed was spread with a quilt in a spectacular peacock design; the bolster covers each had a smaller peacock.

"Just a minute till I change my dress," Mrs. Walters said. "Only Sunday dress I got. Will be by shroud too, just as well to take care of it seein' as how I got to wear it till judgmint day. Ain't folks gonna look funny in all them different kinds a styles on that great day? I said so to the preacher. He says to me, well, now, that's true, Miz Walters, as true a thing as anybody ever spoke, but one thing will be the same, the kinds a sins folks has sinned, ain't nothin' new about sinnin'. I smiled at him as if to say truer words have not been spoke than you're utterin' right now, Preacher Moore, but to myself I says, ain't it just like a preacher to turn what you hope is perlite friendly talk to his own means? Me tryin' to have a little joke about clothes and him a turnin' it into sin."

Mrs. Walters seemed to be wrestling with herself in the closet to which she had modestly withdrawn. I heard one shoe hit the floor, then the other. She came out barefoot, in a petticoat with short sleeves in it, and she wore a sunbonnet. "Summer and winter grandmaw and maw wore sunbonnets and what was good enough for them is good enough for me, town or not. I like a sunbonnet and I aim to wear a sunbonnet and if Miz Ruzvelt and all her childern and their childern was to knock on my door I'd say howdy-do to 'em in a sunbonnet."

She climbed into a calico dress and pulled on red felt bedroom shoes. I kept trying to explain what I was there for. She waved me aside and began an unending monologue. I couldn't pierce it; I couldn't halt it.

"You know, I was just thinkin' comin' back home on the street car about the way a body learns things. Now you take September gales. I can recollict years ago just puttin' on a sweater when that cold windy weather would come of a September and sayin' along with everybody else, well, it's time for September gales. Out in the country they wasn't no way to git news like nowadays from the papers and the radio and just almost anybody you pass on the street has got the answer to whatever you want to ast. Them days we didn't know nothin' about them terrible storms like the hurricanes that's here there and everywheres and the tornadoes that blows up. To us was just unlikely weather, put us out a little because we had to wear a sweater and it September. Why, could be four or five thousand dead in them hurricanes and we didn't know beans about it. All it was to us was puttin' on a little extry clothin' in the daytime and a little extry beddin' at night."

"Mrs. Walters, I'd like to ask you—"

She didn't hear me.

"People don't seem to have fun no more. Looks like they just lost their sense a enjoymint. Law, of a Sunday we usta fry us up two or three fryers, packed our dinner in a shoe box and taken us a all day excursion."

There was no escape. Mrs. Walters's words washed around me, drowning me. Twelve o'clock came and went and still I listened.

"And looks like folks don't have time to be ladies and gentlemen no more. Now you take grandmaw, was about the greatest lady that ever lived. Not the grandmaw I just mentioned that wore sunbonnets but paw's maw. Lord, you wouldn't a catched her in no sunbonnet. Usta josh her about the only time anybody could remember her not bein' a lady. Was like this. Law, they'd say. Such a lady. So refined, so proper, would blush if you so much as belched in her presence,

don't see how she ever got in bed with a man though
they's proof and to spare seein' as how she had thirteen childern. Though grandpaw when that subject
was mentioned just said looked like she enjoyed it as
well as the next one and he oughta know seein' as how
she was his fourth wife. Anyways Sherman was a
comin'. He'd been messin' around way up in north
Georgia and looked like he meant business. Grandmaw didn't live right in Atlanta, the old place was
somewheres clost by. Refugeed to Macon, I think it
was, maybe wasn't Macon, places and names don't
matter to me no longer, I've forgot them long ago.
Anyways they left their fine house that was clost to
Atlanta and refugeed. Of course like most folks after
the war they didn't have nothin'. Had to grub just like
maw's folks. Mighty big comedown. Anyways after
Sherman went on into South Carolina, I think it was,
then marched on down to Savannah, somewheres in
between that time paw's folks come on back. Well,
the house was spared if you want to call it spared. The
Yankees had used it for barracks or headquarters or
some such. So grandmaw upstairs and downstairs here
she went prancin' to see what the Yankees had done
to the house. Others was so glad to be back they just
set on the porch. Well, all of a sudden they heared a
yell come outa grandmaw and she run to the head of
the stairs and screamed down to them and said well,
the Yankees has used paw's room for a outhouse,
—— all over the place."

Mrs. Walters leaned low and whispered the word
softly. "Yes, ma'am, grandmaw said that. Them

Yankees"—Mrs. Walters whispered again— "—— all over paw's room."

Mrs. Walters was wafted by the memory of her grandmother's scatology to a place where I couldn't reach her. I looked helplessly at my watch. My mind frenziedly reviewed all the lectures I had heard, all the notes I had taken, all the articles I had read on How to Terminate an Interview. Nothing helped. I didn't want to desecrate her reminiscences but I must speak.

My voice came in a shout. "I've got to review your case, Mrs. Walters. I've got to get back to the agency. The deadline was at twelve. It's after that now."

"What's that?" she said.

"You get Old Age Assistance. We have to send in a report on you this month."

"But Mrs. Betts that's got my case was just out here three days ago."

"I know. But she's sick and didn't get to finish it It's got to be done again."

"Well, why didn't you say so? I had no idear that's what you come for. I thought you was one of them drummer ladies or one of them women that sets down and says now do you use so and so. I can't buy nothin', hate just to be sayin' no all the time, I don't use nothin', ain't got no money to buy this kind a wash powder and that kind a soap, ain't got no radio. Usta be that tryin' to answer their questions, just sayin' I don't know and no, ma'am, I don't use that stuff, I felt like a lowdown dog, felt like I didn't have a dab a sense, so I says if I just talk along afore they start their riggermarole they'll see I got a little gumption.

"Now then for the Lord's sake, let's git right on with this. Start right in astin' me about my budget."

⊂⊇   ⊂⊇   ⊂⊇

MRS. WALTERS's review got in two hours after the deadline. I had a Coca-Cola and some peanut butter crackers for lunch at my desk; then went down to Files to see if I could find Charles Williams's case.

The Chief of Files, Mrs. Alden, was kind about telling me their routine; the marking of master files to show whether a case is open or closed; how a case is reopened; how the various divisions turn in their cards when a case is closed. I asked about the case of Charles Williams. She went to the master cards; his name wasn't there.

I thanked Mrs. Alden. That was that; there was no Charles Williams case. I had done what I promised Mr. Lawrence, I had tried to find a case that didn't exist.

Mrs. Alden answered the telephone; we had finished with each other. Miss Sams, the Statistical Clerk, came over to me with the air of a saboteur, a conspirator, someone with contraband to dispose of cheap.

"I heard you all talking," she said. "I've been in this place too long to be fooled by their perfect filing system. Tell me what you want."

I told her.

Miss Sams now turned into a magician. She pulled a stack of cards out of her desk. "This is my own count and these are my own cards," she said. "Charles Williams. An Old Age case, number 109-559-A. Williams is a fairly common name, so I put down his address." She told me a number on Capitol Avenue.

"But I don't understand," I said. "His case isn't anywhere. There's no record of it anywhere. Not in master files. Not in our section."

"I told you I don't trust their perfect system. The case may turn up days from now or months from now. They claim never to have lost a case. What's the difference in losing one and not being able to find one when you need it? Though it is a little funny that there's no record anywhere, not even in the master file. But anything can happen at this agency. Anything."

When I went back to the office everyone was leaving for coffee, even Miss Reeves.

"Come on," Bea said to me.

"No thanks," I said.

"Look, you need coffee," Smitty said.

"Please," Gwen insisted.

"I'm sorry," I said, "but I can't. I finally found the Charles Williams case. I mean I found out where he lives. I want to go see him."

No one made any comment; no one shared my excitement that his case really did exist. We all got in the elevator together; we didn't say anything. I didn't look at anyone; I didn't want to see the face of my friend who had killed; I didn't dare look up, there was danger that I might discover the eyes of the one who had waited for me in my darkened rooms, who had jolted me from sleep and whispered threats; I didn't want to see the hands that had shoved Miss Fitzpatrick and had sent Mr. Ricks to the hospital.

They said good-bye to me and crossed the street to go to Eddie's; I walked on up to Mitchell Street to get the Capitol Avenue car.

The address was one of the large rooming-houses that filled the block. I knocked at the door with the head of my umbrella. No one answered. I pushed against the door; it gave unwillingly, sticking at the bottom; with another shove I bolted into a dark hall. Plaster had fallen, leaving great pockmarks on the ceiling. I tapped on the front door to the left.

A man came out holding a tomato can. He spat in it.

"I want to see Mr. Charles Williams, please."

"Ain't no Charles Williams here," he said. "I been livin' here four year and ain't never been no Charles Williams here. Been a coupla of John Williams and a Andrew Jackson Williams. Even been a Thomas Jefferson Williams, but no, ma'am, ain't been no Charles Williams and you can depend on that. Some folks has got minds for figgers and some has got minds for faces. Me, I got a mind for names."

"Are you the landlord? Do you have charge of this place?"

"Do I have charge? Can't say as I do. A woman runs it. I'm just a roomer but they ain't nothin' that gits by me. And if I say they ain't no Charles Williams livin' here they ain't."

"May I see the landlady, please?"

"You can see her but the point is can she see you? She started drinkin' beer a while ago and I wouldn't be wantin' to risk a bet as to whether her eyes is still in focus. She's in the first room at the head of the stairs."

He motioned with the tomato can; spit from it splashed onto the floor. His voice trailed after me up the creaking stairs. "But whether she can see you or not dependin' on how much beer she's got inside her she can't manufacture nobody by the name of Charles Williams and you might just as well save yore breath astin' her because nobody by that name never lived here."

From the closed door a voice called out gaily to me to come in. The landlady sat at a table near a fire; she seemed cheerful and quite pleasant; no buzz from the beer showed. Four empty beer-bottles nestled like affectionate kittens around her feet.

"I wanted to see Mr. Williams," I said. "Somebody downstairs told me you're the landlady."

"Whoever said that was right," she said and bowed. "Now which Mr. Williams was you innerested in seein'? I got several."

"Mr. Charles Williams."

Her fuzzy hair hung down to her shoulders; from somewhere in its muss she pulled two hairpins; she gathered her hair up in a knot and jabbed the two pins in it.

"He don't live here," she said.

"Has he moved?"

"He ain't never lived here." She fluffed some hair over her forehead and produced some imitation bangs.

"He gets a check from our agency every month. It's mailed to this address."

She poured beer into a glass, carefully without a head, the way I like to see it poured. She sensed approval.

"I wish you'd have some of this, though of course I know you can't drink on the job." She took a great gulp, leaving the glass three-fourths empty.

"Now about this here Mr. Williams. His check comes here but his daughter comes by for it. He aims to move here as soon as he gets well. His daughter pays his rent. Ain't but four dollars a month. Not much. But four dollars is four dollars. Just a little old room. Ain't nothin' in it but a bedstid and a table and a oil stove. You can see for yourself if you want to."

She set the beer bottles aside and got up. "Yeah, his daughter come and taken this room for him, said she loved her father but he wanted to be by hisself, vowed and declared he wasn't gonna live with no relatives. This daughter told me her name, Mrs. something or other, but I didn't get it right off and I ain't the kind that says beg pardon what is your name, then asts folks to spell it, like when you give your name you've got to be held accountable for it. Was just a common name. Anyhow she paid for the rent in advance, then come by in about two weeks and said her father had fell, wasn't nothin' serious but she was goin' to keep him with her for the time bein' and would I hold his mail and she'd come get it. I said sure, wasn't nothin outa my pocket and was little enough favor seein' as how I was rentin' that old back room to her father and him not even there. That room ain't been rented since old man Smith died in it three year ago Christmas Day. Seems indecent to die on the Lord's birthday but old man Smith never was one to accommodate nobody, not even the Lord."

"How long have checks been coming here for Mr. Williams?"

I had thought we were going downstairs to see the room; instead she walked over to an icebox and took out another bottle of beer.

"I'd say seven or eight months, maybe longer."

She opened the beer; again I watched her deft way of pouring it.

"May I see the room?"

"Sure. Just let me finish this. Don't want it to get flat."

The beer was gone in the twinkling of an eye. She patted the empty bottle lovingly and said: "God bless, keep, spare and multiply every brewer in the country."

"Come on, Miss what you may call it, I'll show you Mr. Williams's room."

We ambled down the unsteady stairs, through the hall to a back porch; the wind cut us as we walked into the small room, which must have been intended for a pantry or storage of some kind; it was small and dark, crowded with a cot and table and stove, and lighted by a small slit of a window high up in the ceiling.

There was nothing about it to tell what kind of man Mr. Williams was.

"Did his daughter ever bring any of his belongings?"

"Not a thing. Not even as much as a pocket handkerchief."

I walked around in the room, pushed myself between the cot and table to get to the stove, as if to conjure up Mr. Williams. I thought the landlady looked heavenward to try to help me, then I realized she was gazing upstairs toward her room, rapt with the idea of more beer.

"Well, thank you so much," I said. "I hope I haven't bothered you."

I walked ahead of her to the front door. She seemed fat but she leaped up the stairs with a dancer's grace. I was about to go. She called to me from upstairs, her hand fondling a bottle of beer. "Look, hon, may not be nothin'. Just struck me though. Mr. Williams's check was due a week ago and it didn't come. Postman won't give that check to nobody but me. Nobody but me knows the arrangemint with Mr. Williams's daughter. I don't talk my business with nobody, not when the walls is as thin as these is and the ears is as long as grows on the people in this house. Postman knows and I know he's supposed to deliver it in the hands of the one it's addressed to but he can trust me. And Mr. Williams's daughter didn't come by neither to see about it, so I reckon it didn't rile her up none, it not comin' this time."

I thanked her again and said good-bye again.

I heard her open another beer bottle; the cap hopped down the stairs and rolled past me.

She called out once more. "Hon, you've got a mighty peculiar job. Lord knows, I oughtn't to be the one to talk. The roomin'-house business is mighty peculiar too. Come on by sometime when you ain't on duty and we can have a fine time swappin' stories. I've always got a plenty of beer on hand."

⊂⊐ ⊂⊐ ⊂⊐

THE wind swept on in its relentless, determined way. I was weary, utterly tired; I wanted to sit down on the steps of the rooming house and let the wind blow me from the face of the earth. Weeping took more energy than I had or I would have cried and let my tears dissolve me.

I dragged myself down the steps of the house where Charles Williams didn't live but where a room too dismal and cold for any kind of living was being rented to him.

Someone passed me and stopped.

"Why, it's Miss Wallace," a woman said.

I tried to smile and say hello. It was a client; I could have remembered her name if I hadn't been so tired.

"You look like a bar of soap after a hard day's washin'. You look like you lost yore last friend. Well," she said, leaving, "I reckon I better be moseyin' on. Looks like you oughta be gettin' on too. Sure looks like this wind is just gonna chap and shrivel us all."

Digging in my bag for carfare and waiting at a car stop took too much energy and planning; I walked toward the agency.

At Garnett Street an automobile stopped. Gwen called me to get in and ride with her. Cars honked behind her; there was a conspiracy everywhere to complicate my life. I had wanted to be alone, to walk back to the agency; it was simpler, I supposed, to be an automaton. I did as I was told and got in with Gwen.

Gwen said: "You look dead."

I was getting used to such remarks.

"I am awfully tired," I said.

In front of the office she said: "Why don't you come home with me for supper? There won't be much but it'll save you cooking or standing in line downtown. I'll take you home early."

"I'd love it," I said, and meant it. I didn't have to manufacture a response that time.

"I've got to buy some groceries," she said. "I'll let you out and we can meet in the parking lot in half an hour."

Upstairs in the office everyone was waiting for five o'clock; the deadline was over, the reviews were in, at least one day we would quit on time. I wasn't the only one who was tired; they all seemed weary; they all moved slowly; the lights shone on them unkindly, making furrows of faint lines. They apparently decided that five o'clock was lurking outside, hiding from them; at ten minutes to, they all left.

I telephoned Mr. Lawrence and told him about my visit to try to find Charles Williams.

"You sound so tired," he said.

"I am tired."

"This about Mr. Williams is exciting. Doesn't it excite you?" His enthusiasm was genuine but not contagious; I couldn't answer yes. "Is it customary to have a check sent to an address when the person doesn't live there?"

"It's against regulations unless permission has been given."

"Was permission given to Mr. Williams?"

"I don't know. His record isn't around."

"How long has the check been going to him?"

"The landlady couldn't be exact. A number of months, though."

"Isn't there some way you can find out exactly?"

"I suppose the Accounting Department knows."

"See what you can find out from them."

In the Accounting Department Mrs. Farrell had put on her hat; she was pulling on her gloves. When she saw me she pulled off her gloves. "Jane, why does everyone have to have something at the last minute? I'll miss my ride home."

"I'm sorry," I said. "But it's very important. I want to know how long Charles Williams has been getting Old Age Assistance." I gave her the case number.

She twirled the combination of the safe; she tugged

at ledgers, and pounded them against her desk, making an exaggerated show of work, in the way most people do when they think they're being put upon.

"Mr. Williams is dead," she said, as if it served us right.

"Dead?"

"Yes, he died this month. The fourth to be exact. The form canceling his grant says that verification was made through a death notice in the Atlanta *Constitution*."

"How long had he been getting a grant?"

Her fingers shuffled through forms. "Since January of this year."

I thanked her and told her I'd put the ledgers back. She grabbed her pocketbook, knitting-bag, and a sack of candy from Woolworth's, and said: "Excuse me, but you look ghastly." As if it would cure me she stuffed the sack of candy in my hand. "You ought to go home and go to bed at once," she said and trotted out the door.

I telephoned Mr. Lawrence again. Before I could tell him what I had found out about Mr. Williams's grant he said: "You sound tired to death."

"I sound tired. I look tired. I am tired. I wish everyone would stop reminding me."

"You should go home and go to bed."

"That's the second time someone has told me that in the last two minutes."

"Well, do something about it. Now then, what did you find out from the Accounting Department?"

"Mr. Williams is dead. He died on the fourth of

this month. His death was verified by a notice in the *Constitution*. He was getting the maximum grant, as much as we ever pay. Thirty dollars a months."

"You told me how you figure budgets. Do many people get that much?"

"Very few."

"You say he was paying four dollars a month rent?"

"That's what the landlady told me." I held the notes I had made in the Accounting Department. My inept mind noticed something it should have noticed sooner. "Well," I said. "That's strange."

"What's strange?"

"I just realized it. Mr. Williams should have been my case. His check went to Capitol Avenue. That's in my district. His check has always gone there. There's been plenty of time to transfer him to me."

"Did you look in your own card file when you asked the others to see if they had the case?"

"Of course. I haven't had his case. I'm sure of that."

"You've told me this before. Please tell me again. How do you open an Old Age Assistance case? How does anyone get a grant?"

"He has to apply. Sign an application. We have to verify his age and his need. You verify age in the usual way. Need by talking with his children and people who know his circumstances. We check property records, clear with the banks for savings and checking accounts. Then we figure up a budget and if funds are available the applicant gets a grant."

"Does it take long?"

"There can be delays of one kind and another. But

if everything goes along all right a grant can be paid within a month."

"Have a good supper," he said. "And expect a telephone call from me later."

"You mean—"

"I mean I want to check on a few points. I know you don't care for Sherlock Holmes but I must hang up on something he said—it's not what we know, but what we can prove."

"Do you mean you know who killed Mrs. Patch?"

"I think so. Now I must prove it."

THE house welcomed us. Gwen entered reverently, as if she were a chatelaine entrusted with a great château, knowing the intricate history of its structure and the painstaking craftsmanship that went into each fine piece of furniture. She performed with dedication and love the ceremony of returning home, switching on lamps, drawing curtains, touching flower pots to see if they had enough water.

In the living-room I sat down on a red velvet love-seat near the fireplace and hugged my shivering body. "I'm freezing," I said.

Gwen knelt and lighted the fire. "It is chilly," she said. "I'll go turn up the furnace."

I heard her about her duties; my tired brain still insisted that she acted in a hushed, devout way, almost as if she prepared an altar for a sacrifice. She came back soon carrying a decanter and glass. She set these on a table near me.

"I believe sherry's your drink," she said. She poured some and left me.

I picked up the glass and turned it around in my hands. The warmth of the first sip encouraged me; I drank the rest quickly and poured more.

Gwen came back with her hair piled high on her head. On Monday at the staff party as I had watched her in her house she seemed like a little girl playing grownup; now she was entirely grown, quite in command. We watched the fire while she drank a cocktail and I kept on with sherry. Then she said: "Would you like some music while I'm in the kitchen?"

The sherry made me amiable and agreeable to any suggestion. "Thank you," I said. "Thank you very much. I'd like to listen to some music. How thoughtful of you. How kind."

The music cut into my gratitude, drowning out the words just as they were about to gush. The music sounded very like Chopin or Wieniawski or maybe Debussy; I wasn't listening closely because the sherry and I didn't really care.

Luxury surrounded me; I sank into it. In front of me was a fire that wasn't necessary because there was heat from the furnace. The flames reflected on the satin upholstery of the chairs and on the highly waxed floors, coating their richness, making them doubly luxurious. I patted the silky velvet of the loveseat as if it were the soft hide of some lovely animal. All this beauty existed because a child who had known poverty had grown up and found a way to write and so had found everything she thought she wanted, even a job that fed her imagination so there would be no end to her stories. All day long she walked in and out of disease-infested, rat-infested houses and came home to this. For an instant the world's contrasts sickened me; I pulled my hand from the loveseat as if I touched a cancer, and moved it toward the sherry glass; it seemed strange that the glass was empty. I filled it. As I drank I gave myself a brief, scathing lecture. "Jane Wallace, my noble one," I said to myself, "your censure is envy. Gwen works hard; she does wonderful things with her money; she doesn't waste it on cheap, ostentatious junk. She goes to people who revere beauty and fine workmanship and buys what they have. She contributes lavishly to all the community funds, all the hospital funds; she works like fury night and day; she's kind, she's generous, she saw that you were tired to death and offered you her hospitality." Mentally I applauded my speech and agreed that it was accurate; I ended the speech by insisting that I must stop being a shrew that very instant.

I looked up to see Gwen smiling at me; her skirt and blouse were covered in a blue organdy apron, the exact color of her eyes.

"Everything's ready," she said.

We passed through the large dining-room to a breakfast-room furnished in small fat sensuous Victorian chairs upholstered in pink taffeta, a table covered in pale pink damask, a miniature cabinet full of milk glass; our feet mired in a deep green carpet; the bay window was filled with white geraniums in white pots. I shook the table gently as I tried to draw my chair closer.

Gwen said: "You look exhausted."

"I am exhausted," I said, wondering how many times I'd said it since late afternoon. "I can't remember being so tired. And maybe I've had too much sherry."

"What you need is food."

She heaped a plate and handed it to me.

The ham was fine, the salad excellent, the biscuit wonderful, and there was no word for the way the chiffon pie bewitched my palate.

We finished with coffee; sometime during my second cup my chin bobbed on my collar. I whispered: "I'm dead tired." I didn't have to have someone say it first; I didn't need any coaching that time.

"I've got some benzedrine I take sometimes when I sit up late to write. Would you like some?"

"No," I said. "But I do think I should get home right away."

"Maybe you'd like to take a nap here. That is, if my typing won't bother you. I could wake you whenever you like."

"I'd rather go home," I said. "Can you take me now?" I wanted to say something about hating to leave her with all the dishes to wash; I didn't seem to be able to say it.

Outside the wind felt good on my face; I rolled the car window down as far as it would go.

In a short while Gwen nudged me and said: "Here we are. Can I help you out?"

"No, I'm fine." I said it emphatically but my legs wouldn't take me anywhere. I clung to the car. Gwen jumped out and put her arm around my waist.

Upstairs in my living-room she said: "I think you need a doctor. Let me call one. Let me stay with you tonight."

"That's silly," I said. "I'm simply tired. All I need is rest. I've had a good meal and three glasses of sherry. And after all, it's been a hectic week."

"Are you sure there isn't anything I can do?"

"No, thank you." Then I remembered that Mr. Lawrence planned to telephone me. "Maybe after all I'll take some benzedrine, that is if you brought it with you."

"I may have some in my bag. I'll see in a moment."

Gwen had somehow taken over my rooms in the way she had taken over her own house. She brought cream and put it on my face; she uncovered the couch and made it ready for bed; she found my pajamas and brought them to me in the bathroom; she took the decanter from the mantel and put it near the couch. She looked in her bag; out of a tiny pink box she took two white pills and set them near the decanter. Then she tucked me in.

"Are you sure you don't want me to stay?"

"I'm sure," I said.

"Don't take the benzedrine. It'll be much better if you go right off to sleep."

She said good night very softly and closed the door.

I heard her walk down the stairs; the hall door closed quietly, those were her steps on the gravel of the driveway; her car started; I watched its lights circle my ceiling as the car made a turn.

Gwen was gone.

I dozed. I waked, scolding myself, remembering Mr. Lawrence's telephone call might come soon. Sleep sprang at me, overpowering me. I sat up. I dodged sleep, refusing to be its victim. I reached for the benzedrine; the pills hung in my throat. I needed water but water was far away; I picked up the decanter and washed the benzedrine down with sherry.

I lay back on the bed, waiting.

And then soon I knew it was not Mr. Lawrence's telephone call that kept me waiting. I was waiting for death. My door was unlocked and I could not get to it to close death out; and death was coming toward me now on quiet feet, perhaps inching along, perhaps taking bold strides; no matter, death would be with me in a little while. I whimpered to reject death and then I did not whimper. I was sinking deep inside nothingness, being welcomed wherever I was going softly, with the gentleness of tender fingers on a tired, aching head. Death was entering, as a lover, kind, generous, soothing me, caressing me, fondling me. Life was the enemy, calling me back to its stupid, unendurable tasks, trying to cajole me into resistance, trying to tear me from the sweet peace and inaction of death. Life with its harshness had nothing to offer so good as death's soft calm.

With the last of my consciousness I smiled at death.

⊂⇥ ⊂⇥ ⊂⇥

FIGURES tugged at me, hands pulled, lifted. I begged them to leave me in peace, I wanted to get down on my knees to them, to grovel so that they would know I wanted to be let alone. A dark figure hovered over me; it was Andrew. I smiled at him, remembering his kindness, his gentle hands that wiped away tension; he would know what I wanted; he would make the others go, his strong, kind hands would persuade them to leave me. Instead he reached for me, made me stand; he was on their side, my enemy, urging me to do the impossible, to walk, to move, not to fall asleep.

A cloud rescued me, blotting out Andrew's face, all the faces and voices, the stupid words ordering me to do miracles. I lay on gossamer, softness enveloped me in cotton smoothness.

The cloud withdrew, dumping me again among enemies. I saw faces; I was surrounded. At my feet Gwen was bent in grief, rocking back and forth, saying she shouldn't have left me. Bea sat quietly in a chair looking at me. Without emotion I thought that she must be waiting for my death mask. Margy cried; her tears washed down her face, leaving it ugly, yet Ted glanced down at her as if she were the most beautiful woman alive. Smitty sat on the floor; her hands embraced her legs, her body was pushed forward so that her head rested on her knees. Peg leaned over me. Mrs. Martin touched my forehead. I looked again, not believing it; yes, Miss Reeves was there too, smiling at me, she was the only one who smiled.

I felt weak, breathing was too difficult. I tried to do less of it. I wanted to ask where I was and then I saw the portraits of the children over the chest; the little daughter of Madame Vigee-Lebrun still looked at herself with wonder in the mirror she held; Don Manuel Osorio De Zuniga still stood holding his bird by a string. I was home.

The moment was awkward; I didn't know what to say and so I said hello. Peg hovered even more efficiently, Gwen sat up, Smitty unbent herself and turned around, Bea still sat quietly, Mrs. Martin lifted her hand from my forehead, Miss Reeves's wan smile became friendly and warm, the warmest I had ever seen on her sad face; Margy and Ted grabbed each other as if I were their favorite child showing signs of living after all. I was assaulted by are you all right and how do you feel in many tones and voices.

"I'm sleepy," I said. My mouth opened in a yawn; before I closed it Peg had rushed at me and ladled strong black coffee down my throat. I went to sleep at once.

When I waked again the room was empty except for Peg and a young man; they seemed to be plotting.

The man said: "She's all right. There's nothing to worry about. She won't have any ill effects." His exit was quick and noiseless.

"You heard the doctor," Peg said. "You're fine. Everything's fine. I'm going to lie down and take a nap." She threw a cushion on the floor and stretched out. "Thank God tomorrow's Sunday. We can all have a nice rest."

"Then today's Saturday," I said.

"Yes, today's Saturday."

"And yesterday was Friday."

Peg smiled as if I were a cretin showing unexpected talent for logic. "That's right. Yesterday was Friday."

I slept and waked again to find Peg standing in the middle of the floor, her face distorted, full of pain. She didn't know I watched her; she shook her head, as if to erase some awful fact, and whispered: "No, no, no." I made a great show of waking up. Peg forced her face back to its usual serenity; she was smiling when I looked at her.

"Are you all right?"

"I'm fine," I said.

"Then I must go."

I wanted to ask what had happened to me, what had happened to her; she dashed out before I could say anything. Her rapidly moving feet seemed barely to touch the stairs, as if disdaining them.

It was getting dark; rain began to fall, it struck belligerently at the windows. I got up and went to the kitchen. A desperate, raging hunger possessed me. I opened split-pea soup and chicken soup. I ate half a loaf of bread and a can of cold pork and beans while I waited for the soup to heat; I upended the bowl to get the last bite of pork and beans; then I started on the scalding chicken soup.

The clock in the kitchen said quarter to five. I

sopped bread in the bowl to get the last of the chicken soup; then I gulped the split pea soup. At last my hunger was gone; in its place came curiosity, as raging and desperate as the hunger had been. I wondered what had happened to me; I dragged at my memory. Gwen had brought me home the night before, Friday night; when she left I had felt danger, death was reaching for me; then I had felt peace. I waked up to see faces I loved around me. I slept and waked again to find only Peg; I dozed and, waking, had seen Peg in distress. The week rushed back with all its frightful memories; I saw Mrs. Patch dead, I saw Mary hanging, I saw Miss Fitzpatrick sprawled at the foot of the stairs.

Then I shut out all the memories but one: Mr. Lawrence had promised to telephone me last night and he hadn't. I must find out why. I dialed his number.

"How good it is to hear your voice," he said. "Are you all right?"

"I'm fine. But I don't know what's happened to me. And I was wondering if you really did learn who the murderer was."

"Yes. And last night I tried to telephone you. But you didn't answer. I knew most of our mystery then. Now I know everything."

"Everything?"

"Yes. And I want to tell you. Can you come over?"

"As soon as I bathe and dress."

"Good."

I was about to say good-bye when he spoke again.

"Please don't read any of the late papers. Just as a favor to me. I want to tell you about it all."

When I hung up the receiver dread took hold of me and wouldn't let me move. I had no idea what caused it and then I realized I didn't want to know what Mr. Lawrence knew. Let him keep his hateful knowledge; I didn't want to know the name of my friend who had done murder, the friend who only a few hours before had been in my room solicitious, worried over what had happened to me, loving me, wanting me well. My friends were all generous and good and kind. I detested, I was revolted by the idea of anything or anyone who would try to prove they weren't.

Yet I had promised Mr. Lawrence I would go to his house and I must. I turned the tap on slowly so that the water fell in an unwilling dribble to the tub; from the cabinet I dug out some bath crystals I never used and dumped them in the bath water. I welcomed the time it took them to dissolve; anything to delay my visit to Mr. Lawrence, anything to put off learning what he knew.

I DRESSED with studied, determined leisure; I concentrated with an idiot's fascination on pushing cuticles back, getting stocking seams precisely straight, brushing my coat meticulously as if it were a horse being curried for a show. The moment came when all the tasks were done; nothing more could be trumped up.

A streetcar waited for me at the corner as if it had been ordered. The trip to town was the quickest I had ever made, everything conspired to hurry me. Downtown when I got off the car two newsboys waved early editions of the Sunday papers. Mercifully the funnies covered the headlines; their gay pages hid the news. The paper-sellers yelled their gibberish; I ran as I heard them shout read all about it, even though the rest of their chant was unintelligible.

Rain seemed to have seeped through the pavements, crumbling them, everyone walked in slush, umbrellas mushroomed everywhere; mine leaned heavily against the wind, then reached an impasse. I shut the umbrella and walked frowning against the wind and the rain. The island at Five Points was unprotected from the rain and crowded with people waiting for streetcars; I walked to another stop. The people waiting there pulled themselves in, they seemed to try to shrink so there would be room for me to stand with them in the narrow shelter of a store doorway; the proprietor scowled at us, blaming us for his lack of customers, as if we barricaded them from his matchless bargains.

I let one car pass. I wasn't ready for the end of my journey. Soon another car followed it, in a delirium of unconcern that the rain made shambles of schedules. There was no transfer in the pocket where I always stuck them; I had forgotten to get one. I moaned at the extravagance of having to pay an extra fare.

On the seat in front of me a man settled down with his Sunday paper; he spread out in the luxury of a whole seat to himself; the funnies slipped, revealing huge black words: MURDERER CONFESSES. His back bent avidly over the paper, hiding everything but the edges that trembled with the streetcar's vibration.

The words hammered away at my consciousness. Murderer Confesses. I dismissed the harrowing words. I watched a fat little girl on a street corner strain for her mother's hand; I saw umbrellas collide, become entangled, I saw brief indignation flare as automobiles jolted by splashing people.

I got off a block earlier and walked slowly to Mr. Lawrence's; yet all my delays meant nothing, they added up to nothing; I might have rushed headlong to his house.

I was knocking at his door.

Andrew welcomed me. From his bed Mr. Lawrence asked: "Are you all right?"

I nodded, not wanting to speak. I was waiting to learn of a malignancy; somehow I had to shove back the fateful moment. Mr. Lawrence understood; he made appropriate remarks about the weather.

"There's coffee, if you'd like some," he said.

I drank the coffee without talking.

At last Mr. Lawrence said: "What we're going to talk about has happened. Nothing we do or say can change it. You've known all along anyway who it was. You may have refused to look at it, but you knew."

"Of course I didn't know."

"But you must have. All I knew and all I worked on was what you told me."

I could ask the question then. My lips no longer hated it; my brain was ready to accept it. "Who? Tell me. Who was it?"

"Gwen."

I felt nothing; there was no surprise, no unbelief. "How? Why? I don't see."

"That was the problem, finding out why. It was simple to learn who it was, but why? A girl with everything. I mean everything she wanted. The only one of you who had everything, the only one who had planned her life and had her plans work out. You'll have plenty of time to think through the details. I'll tell you only a few things. We were looking for someone who could take advantage of whatever happened to her or around her. Gwen had been desperately poor as a child. That hadn't made her bitter but ambitious. She found a job she liked when she grew up. From that job she got material to write—whether she used actual happenings or not, her job stimulated her, gave her incidents, facts, atmosphere for writing. She took advantage of it all. She got the house she wanted, the furniture, all the possessions she longed for. Then something happened. The war. It affected everything. Even, I decided after I'd read a number, the kinds of stories published by confession magazines. Gwen told you her house was paid for by illegitimate births, illicit love, abortions, but that afternoon when you were caught in the rain at a client's house and spent your time reading confessions you didn't find any illegitimate births or abortions. They weren't publishing stories about illicit love any more. They had been publishing that kind almost entirely. I could tell from old issues. I decided that Gwen hadn't been able to write the new type of story.

"The night you came here from Grady. Remember? Andrew didn't answer the door as soon as you knocked. Well, he was putting away the confession magazines I'd been reading.

"Then all that reading of confession stories didn't help at all because you had seen Gwen with checks amounting to eight hundred dollars from publishers of confession magazines. My theory wasn't working.

"So for a short time I left Gwen and considered everybody else. The rest of you had a motive. You all hated Mrs. Patch. Each of us hates many persons. We don't usually kill them. But in this case someone had been murdered and it must have been someone who hated Mrs. Patch. As I say, it might have been any one of you.

"Then I began to think about all the things that had happened. Mary had committed suicide. I was willing to go along with the police and accept Mary's suicide note. But you and Bea wouldn't let me. Your reactions wouldn't. You didn't believe it. Bea especially didn't believe it. I told you before I believed Bea knew who had murdered Mrs. Patch. Bea with her amazing insight, the way she can see souls, the way she paints souls—she must have known. Ask her sometime. I'm sure she knew it was Gwen.

"I've told you I think everyone is capable of

murder. But under the circumstances Mary couldn't have murdered Mrs. Patch. She was obsessed by grief.

"To get back to the things that happened. There were the attacks on Miss Fitzpatrick and Mr. Ricks. They were stupid. There was nothing wholehearted about them. No one was really hurt. No one was intended to be hurt badly, simply frightened a bit. Miss Fitzpatrick and Mr. Ricks knew nothing about the murder. But you—the moment you mentioned Charles Williams you were in danger. You couldn't find his record. Yet you remembered seeing it. I wondered if it could have been destroyed. But why? You said even if you found it it wouldn't have anything in it but the usual proof of age and need. Then finally you found Charles Williams's address and made a visit to that delightful beer-drinking woman. You learned that Mr. Williams's daughter called for the check; her father was ill, she said. You had told me how you figured budgets. Charles Williams's rent was four dollars a month. How could his budget be figured so that he got the maximum amount of thirty dollars? Then you checked further and found out that he was dead. He had lived and died and apparently no one had seen him. He had died on the fourth of the month, you said.

"Well, you told me all those things last night. And I said I knew who the murderer was. I had to check to prove it. I knew Gwen did it because who else would have been awake or stayed awake until two thirty to threaten you over the telephone? Gwen was up late writing. Who else would have taken advantage of the note Mary left? I was positive it was Gwen.

"Then for the proof. Last night after I talked with you I telephoned the *Constitution* and asked about the death notice of Mr. Williams. There had been none, neither on the fourth nor on any other day this month. I telephoned the *Journal*. It was the same. No record at all. Mr. Williams hadn't died, I became convinced, because he couldn't die; he hadn't ever lived. But every month a check had been made out in his name and every month it had been called for at the rooming-house.

"Whoever did that must have been desperate for money. But I was working with the assurance that it was Gwen and she had plenty of money apparently. I thought of her love for antiques. I telephoned one of my friends who is a dealer. Yes, he had a pleasant relationship with Gwen. She was one of his best customers. There had been a time about a year ago when she couldn't pay for the things she'd bought. He hated to take the pieces back. Gwen loved them, was a real connoisseur, there weren't many like her who truly revered fine craftsmanship. Suddenly, after a lapse of two or three months, she had started making payments. She owed him nothing now, her house needed no more furniture, though she still dropped by often to see what he had and to talk about woods and glass and silver.

"I telephoned another friend—this one a writer—about the confession stories to see if I was right. Yes, there had been a definite change in the kind of story published; editors required a new type, the same style, the same emotion, but different subject matter. The change was caused by the war; magazines mustn't contribute to laxity in morals or juvenile delinquency.

"That was all the checking I needed. There were some gaps. But we had our solution. We knew who our murderer was. And we had proved it. I wanted to talk it over with you, to ask you what we ought to do. I telephoned you as I promised. You didn't answer. For an hour I tried to get you. Then I sent Andrew over. He found you in a coma. He asked what he should do. We telephoned a doctor. We telephoned all your friends; they went to your rooms immediately. Gwen explained to the doctor that you had been to her house for an early supper and had asked her for sleeping pills. She hadn't noticed how many you took. You weren't used to them. You were exhausted. You must have taken too many.

"After several hours you were all right. Peg stayed with you; the others left. I could proceed.

"I telephoned Gwen. I think that was one of the most extraordinary conversations anyone ever had. I told her what I knew. In a very friendly way she filled in the rest. I know what you mean when you say everyone likes Gwen. She's a charming person. Yes, she told me, she had been desperate when the editors stopped buying her stories; she had sold regularly at least one story a week for six years; the editors were still kind, they encouraged her, said they thought she was getting on to the new kind of story, but they rejected everything she sent. She couldn't meet payments on her house or on her furniture. She had to have money. She nearly lost her mind; then she decided to open ten cases for Old Age Assistance grants, each for the maximum amount of thirty dollars a month. She forged all the evidence. She collected each check, using the same story with little variation; sometimes she was a niece, usually a daughter. All the time she considered that the money she was taking was a loan. She had contributed thousands of dollars to charity; as soon as she got the knack of writing the new type of story she would contribute thousands more.

"Then in a few months she was writing stories as easily as ever and making more at them; rates had been increased. She started closing out the ten cases gradually. As soon as the mechanics of closing were completed she destroyed the case records and all the cards in all the files. She didn't dare do all the closings at the same time because Mrs. Patch might get suspicious. Mrs. Patch didn't usually miss a thing. But somehow the closings did get by Mrs. Patch until the last one. That night when she read Charles Williams's case and saw that he lived in your district she knew quite well that there was a discrepancy. You see, Mrs. Patch knew Gwen wouldn't have held a case that belonged to someone else. Not for all those months. Gwen did her share of the work. But no more. She wouldn't keep a case that she could transfer. Mrs. Patch tried to telephone the references Gwen showed in the narrative as verifying Mr. Williams's need and residence. They weren't in the City Directory. She learned from the telephone company that the phone numbers Gwen listed for the references didn't exist.

"So Mrs. Patch accused her. Ted heard her. You know he said he had never heard such abuse. Everything was lost to Gwen. You remember what a rage she got into the night of the party over one coffee cup. What must it have been for her to realize that she was losing everything? I'm sure for a moment she was insane. And in that moment of insanity she killed Mrs. Patch.

"The next night she found Mary. You remember the client you visited about the pajama order said when she telephoned that whoever it was at the agency who talked seemed unwilling to come out unless it was a real emergency. Of course that meant it was Gwen, anxious to get home to write. The rest of you would have gone without any questions. You said Gwen was generous with her money but not with her time. Anyhow when she went into the clothing-room to get the pajamas she saw Mary and the note. She knew, as you all knew, that Mary would have accepted the blame. So she added a line to the note, saying Mrs. Patch's death was an accident. Gwen had been on her way home. She wore gloves and didn't take them off. There were no prints but Mary's on the suicide note.

"She tried to frighten Miss Fitzpatrick and Mr. Ricks. She hadn't meant to hurt them; she just wanted to make them stop talking about Mary's not killing Mrs. Patch. She said Miss Fitzpatrick wouldn't have fallen if she hadn't had too much port.

"Everything was fine until you insisted on finding out about Charles Williams. Gwen followed you in her car, she waited near the rooming-house until you came out, then drove around another way and picked you up. You were dangerous. And she really did try to kill you with an overdose of sleeping pills. They were in the sherry and on the chiffon pie. Most of them she had crumbled in the sugar. She'd forgotten that sometimes you take sugar in your coffee and sometimes you don't. Perhaps that's what saved you. And of course the benzedrine she left with you was really sleeping pills. She even put some in your decanter.

"Her great mistake was in not knowing that I knew what you knew. She was stunned when I telephoned and then she told me everything. She asked what she was to do. There seemed to be no need for your other friends to know that Gwen had tried to kill you. And I saw no reason for a scandal about funds—Gwen had paid back a dozen times the money she had taken. I told her so. How dare anyone judge another? Gwen thanked me for calling and said good-bye.

"Late this morning they found her horribly mangled. She had thrown herself in front of a train, but not quickly enough or efficiently enough to kill herself instantly—there were two hours of agony. She left a note saying she had killed Mrs. Patch; she wrote that the death was accidental. She didn't mention the money she had taken; she didn't mention her attacks on you or Mr. Ricks or Miss Fitzpatrick. She did say that she had added a sentence to Mary's note. Clipped to this statement was her will; she left everything to the children's agencies in town."

I began to weep; I couldn't stop.

Mr. Lawrence pretended not to notice and kept on talking. "I've been thinking of Anthony Berkeley's remarkable *Trial and Error*. You remember in that fine detective story the issue is what person deserves most to be murdered. Everyone decides it should be someone who is making life miserable for a small group. That was the kind of murder Gwen committed. Think of it. Think of the pressure relieved among the staff because of what Gwen did."

For a moment I didn't want to think of death and murder; I wanted to think about life. I wanted to talk about its harshness; I wanted to ask questions I hadn't dared ask before.

"How do you stand it, day after day, being bedridden? Not to be able to move without pain?" I said.

My question didn't embarrass Mr. Lawrence; he smiled; he waited to speak, as if he were seeking for the true answer.

"However we suffer we're in the midst of a miracle. Just this intake of air—breathing, waking, sleeping, the strangeness of dreams. No matter how much pain there is, to live is a miracle. And think how blessed I am. I have you. I have all my friends. Especially Andrew. Think of him. Think of his race. The patience of his race. The goodness. Think of the burdens they have lifted from us. Think of the awful burdens we have placed on them."

"What are we to do?" I said. "What are all of us to do?"

"My dear, you want a simple answer like always vote the straight Democratic ticket. I don't know what we're to do except to love one another and to be patient with one another. To realize that all human beings are so much the same. We mustn't hoard our little secrets and our small dreams and our sins and hopes as if we were different from everyone else. We must recognize our sameness. Above everything, we mustn't give in to hopelessness."

For this night there were no more words to be said. I went to Mr. Lawrence and kissed him. At the front door I did what I had so long wanted to do. I tiptoed and kissed Andrew, I took his hands and held them to my face.

I left the small gracious house and thought with gratitude of it and the two fine men it sheltered. I walked toward the agency.

Across the street from it I stood staring at its darkness. I thought of the three empty desks. I thought of all of us who came and went there, workers and clients. For a little while I wanted to stop thinking.

Someone sauntered by and stood near me. It was Mr. Ricks, on his way home from supper. Together we looked at the agency.

"Miz Cole, my landlady, read me all about it," he said. "Was all on the radio too. That pore Miss Pierce." I didn't answer; my thoughts echoed his. Poor Gwen.

"Well," he said, "I'm mighty proud to see you."

I smiled at him and he smiled back. He walked on by. I watched his tiny courageous figure move away from me. Before he crossed the street he turned slowly and we faced each other once more.

He spoke again. "Last few days if it warn't rainin' the wind was blowin' hard enough to blow us all to Kingdom Come. But it's fairin' up now. Looks to me like we're in for a right good spell of weather."

A NOTE ON THE TYPE
IN WHICH THIS BOOK IS SET

This book is set in Electra, a Linotype face designed by W. A. Dwiggins. This face cannot be classified as either modern or old-style. It is not based on any historical model, nor does it echo any particular period or style. It avoids the extreme contrast between thick and thin elements that marks most modern faces, and attempts to give a feeling of fluidity, power, and speed. The book was composed, printed, and bound by H. Wolff, New York.

Date Due